Bone's Gift

GHOSTS OF ORDINARY OBJECTS

Bone's Gift

ANGIE SMIBERT

BOYDS MILLS PRESS
AN IMPRINT OF HIGHLIGHTS
Honesdale, Pennsylvania

For information about permission to reproduce selections from this book,
please contact permissions@highlights.com.

This is a work of fiction. Names, characters, places, and incidents are products
of the author's imagination or are used fictitiously. Any resemblance to actual
events, locales, or persons, living or dead, is entirely coincidental.

Boyds Mills Press
An Imprint of Highlights
815 Church Street
Honesdale, Pennsylvania 18431
boydsmillspress.com
Printed in the United States of America

ISBN: 978-1-62979-850-9 (hc)
978-1-68437-136-5 (eBook)
978-1-68437-373-4 (pb)
Library of Congress Control Number: 2017949841

First edition
10 9 8 7 6 5 4 3 2 1

Design by T.L. Bonaddio
The type is set in Adobe Garamond Pro.

To the Forever Girl in all of us

1

BONE PHILLIPS FLOATED in the cool, muddy water of the New River up to her eyeballs. The sky above was as blue as a robin's egg, and the sun was the color of her mama's butter-yellow sweater.

Her mother was still everywhere and nowhere Bone looked.

She let herself sink under the water and swam along the river bottom toward shore—toward Will.

In the shallows, her hand brushed against something hard and jagged on the silky river bottom. An image poured over her like cold bathwater. A young boy had hit his head on this rock. He struggled for air. The current grabbed at him—and her, pulling her along back in time. Bone snatched her hand away from the rock and came up for air with a gasp.

Not again.

The object had a story in it. This one wasn't as bad as the first. That one, back in July, had been downright awful. Still, Bone didn't care for the experience one bit. She felt like she'd been tossed into the river to sink or swim. And no one was there to pull her out—except maybe Will.

As Bone stood half out of the water, trembling, eyes bored into her. Will hadn't looked in her direction. He was still fishing from the downed log, lost in his own thoughts. Bone looked up the bank, to the road. Her cousin Ruby straddled her bicycle in one of her store-bought dresses, staring at Bone. Ruby turned away as two girls and a boy rode up on their bikes. The boy pulled Bone's overalls off the nearby branch. Ruby grabbed them back from him and threw them to the ground. The others rode off, laughing. Ruby lingered for a moment. She picked up Bone's clothes from the dirt and hung them back in place. With a shake of her head in Bone's direction, Ruby pushed off after her friends.

Bone ducked back under the brown water and shut her eyes tight. She didn't want to see the long-ago boy hitting his head—or the here-and-now Ruby shaking hers. Bone pushed all the sounds and images down deep where she couldn't hear or see them. Then she pictured tales of princesses, wandering Gypsies, and frontier fighters, flickering in her mind like movies. Those were the stories Bone liked to tell. Those stories calmed her like still waters.

Silent Will Kincaid listened to her stories. His silence was better than most people's conversation. He was like one of those big rocks out in the middle of the river she liked to sun herself on, solid and warm and always there. And her words flowed around him like the burbling waters of the New River.

Bone surfaced next to Will. One of his overall straps dangled down in back. She reached up to tug him into the water, but his hand was already there, waiting to pull her up beside him. He hauled her onto the tree and kept fishing.

Bone stretched herself along the trunk and let the early September sun bake dry her skin and the cut-off long johns and T-shirt she swam in.

The lonesome wail of a train whistle blew as the Virginian wound around the bend on the other side of the river.

"You know that big rock face over yonder?" Bone shouted above the din of the long line of coal cars rattling along the tracks.

Will began to reel in his empty line.

"Well, that was once called Angel's Rest. Jilted lovers used to jump off of it and dash themselves to bits on the rocks below."

Will packed up his fishing gear. Bone knew he had other things on his mind, and they needed to get to the commissary before it closed. Still, she started in on a tale of two fateful lovers. It wasn't the real story. Uncle Ash had told her a mother died trying to save her child. Bone didn't like tales about dead mamas.

As she wound through the end of her story, Will was climbing to the road. Bone scrambled up the bank to where her overalls still hung from a branch, thanks to Ruby. Bone hopped into them, yanking them on over her still-damp underclothes and fastening them as she ran after him.

"And that's why the train whistle sounds so lonesome coming around that bend." Bone caught up with Will, and they walked along the gravel road together not saying another word. She was content in Will's stony silence.

A sound like thunder broke that silence. The skies were clear, and the mines were closed for another day. In the summer, the men worked other jobs, picking fruit or milling lumber, or they hunted, farmed, and fished to put food on the table. Come the first Friday after Labor Day, both the mines and schools opened. So, that sound could mean only one thing. Bone and Will raced up the road, over the train tracks, and into the coal camp.

The thunder grew more deafening as they whipped past the tipple and the mine entrance. The sound couldn't drown out the hoots of Warren "Jake" Lilly as he flew down the black slate pile on a sled made from a scrap of sheet metal no bigger than a hall rug. He hit the dirt and skidded some yards before he spilled out into the grass at Will's feet. Clay Whitaker leapt down from his perch on the timber frame of the tipple, the chute that loaded coal onto the trains. He scratched out the spot where Jake's sled had stopped its forward motion.

"A new record," he declared.

Jake beamed as he knocked the coal dust and dirt from his dungarees.

"Want to give her a try?" He nudged Will. A slow smile dawned over Will's face, and he followed Jake and Clay. It made Bone forget where he'd be going.

The boys climbed the slate pile in giant strides as if they were kings of the hill. Near the top, Will tugged on Jake's sleeve and cocked his head toward Bone. The other boys stopped to consider her.

Jake shrugged.

"She's just a girl." Clay scrambled to the top.

Bone stared at the back of their heads for a moment and reached down for a rock, half intending to hurl it at the back of Clay's fat little head. Instead, she studied its thick veins of black sandwiched by even thicker layers of brown. The stone was more rock than coal. Like her. Her fingertips tingled. A vein of a story ran deep through the rock. But it didn't overwhelm her. It teased her. The story was more like the faraway trickle of a stream, tempting her to come closer. She didn't fall for it.

Bone dug deep in her brain for a better tale. One that would make the boys (and her) laugh. One far from the one in the rock. She latched onto a story her Uncle Ash had told her the last time she was over to Mamaw's house.

"Well, y'all have fun without me," she called after the boys. "I was going to tell you this story I heard about a prank gone terribly wrong." She turned and started to head slowly toward the commissary. "It had mules and outhouses and everything."

She heard them stop. Jake Lilly called out her name. She kept walking.

"All right, come on, then," Clay relented. "It better be a good one."

Bone stuffed the stone in her left pocket and chased up the pile after the boys. She promised to tell the story over a cold drink at the store after they finished. "Loser buys the pop."

Will beat Jake's mark by a few inches.

When her turn came, Bone clung to the metal and dove headfirst onto the rocks. The whang of the sheet metal against stone nearly deafened her, but she could still hear Jake and Clay cheering as she tore down the pile. Sharp edges jabbed at her through the thin metal. The coal whipped by her face. Bone held on tighter and closed her eyes. She was flying down a soft mountain of snow rather than a crag of black rock.

She skidded past Jake's and Will's marks in the dirt and spilled out into the grass by the commissary.

The boys ran down the hill and collapsed in a heap next to her.

"Damn, Bone. Thought you'd killed yourself for sure." Jake had a new respect in his voice.

Clay shook his head as he scraped a fresh line in the dirt. "Another record."

Bone brushed the gravel from her torn overalls. Then she hooked her thumbs in the straps and strutted back toward the slag pile. She was king of the hill.

"Your daddies ought to switch you," a sharp voice rang out from the commissary steps, sending all the boys except Will running. It was Mrs. Mattie Albert, the preacher's wife and, unfortunately, Bone's aunt on her mother's side.

Bone beat the coal dust from her overalls, sending tiny billows of black in her aunt's direction. It wasn't enough to ward her off. In times like this, Bone liked to reflect on Uncle Ash's wise words about his own big sister. He'd always say, "You can't pick your family, but you sure as hell can pick your own nose." He knew that got Aunt Mattie's goat and made Bone smile.

"Laurel Grace Phillips, whatever are we going to do with you?" Her aunt pulled out a compact mirror from her purse and held it up to Bone. "You look like a wild thing. I despair of making a lady of you."

Bone saw long, damp, stringy blond hair. Tanned and freckled skin. Muddy long johns and dusty, torn overalls. She stuck her tongue out at herself.

"No wonder they call you Bone." Mattie Albert snapped her compact closed and put it back in her purse.

Bone couldn't remember exactly when folks started calling her that. It might have been after Mama died. Bone didn't care. She liked her name.

"*Laurel* looks fine, *Amarantha*." Daddy stepped out onto the store's porch with a new pouch of tobacco in hand.

Aunt Mattie stiffened at her given name, as she always did when Bone's daddy called her that. And he always called her that.

"Now, Bay, we all know you've done as well as you could raising Laurel without benefit of a woman's influence, but there comes a time when she's got to lay aside childish things . . ." She slathered it on as thick as Karo syrup. "She has to think about her future. No self-respecting young man will want to marry . . ."

Bone lost track of what her aunt was saying. It was what she always said. Bone had to wear dresses. Act like a lady. Learn to cook and sew. All so she could be a good Christian wife and mother someday. Daddy nodded as Aunt Mattie talked, but he held himself like he was taking a switching and didn't want to let on how much he was feeling it. Bone plunged her hand deep into her pocket. She still had that stone, and it seemed smoother after her journey down the hill. The smooth stone reminded her of a story. David and Goliath. The boy David had chosen five smooth stones from the stream before he faced the Philistine. As she stared at the middle of Mattie Albert's forehead, Bone wished she had a slingshot.

At that moment, Aunt Mattie's voice dropped to a hushed whisper. "You know Willow was about her age when—"

Bone's father flinched ever so slightly. "Bone ain't Willow," he snapped. "And you know my mind on the subject." He stood straight as a rod now, and his look dared her to say another word. "Superstitious nonsense," he muttered.

Bone had no idea what Aunt Mattie was on about, probably something to do with church. Daddy thought everything was superstitious nonsense. Even church.

Aunt Mattie closed her mouth.

It was the only part of her that looked remotely like Bone's mother. Other than that they had nothing in common. Everyone loved Mama. She had a feeling for people, Daddy always said with a sad look in his eye.

The stone in Bone's hand had a thick vein of black coal winding through it like a river. The stone was whispering a story. It was her story, their story—hers, her father's, her mother's, and even her aunt's—running through that rock. The weight of time and loss and the mountains had made it hard.

It was a big vein.

The words of the story grew louder in Bone's head. She closed her eyes and thought about princesses and Gypsy curses and flying rabbits. Anything really but what the object was trying to tell her. When Bone opened her eyes again, her father and aunt were staring at her. Bone could see now that her Aunt Mattie had her mother's eyes.

Unfortunately, those eyes were looking at Bone like she was something that needed fixing.

2

BONE FELT A TUG on her overall strap. It was Will, and she knew what was on his mind. "Daddy, we got to get Will his gear."

Her father took the rock from Bone's hand. He held it up and peered at the thin vein of coal running through the mostly brown stone. "Will, now this here is the kind of stone you don't want in your handcar at the end of the day." He pitched it back toward the slag pile.

Aunt Mattie peered at Bone like she wanted to say it: *bone.* That's what that rock was, the worthless stone that's left behind when the coal's gone. *That was her.* Bone peered back hard at her aunt, daring her to say anything. Mattie looked away.

Will was all ears as he listened, nodding like Daddy'd said the wisest thing on earth. Bone's father was the day shift supervisor at Big Vein Superior Anthracite Mine and soon to be Will's boss. So he'd better listen. Bone didn't want to lose both of them.

"How is *that boy* going to work in the mines?" Aunt Mattie asked.

Bone put her hands on her hips. Will was as smart and as good as anyone. Better than most.

"Hush, Amarantha," Daddy said. "He don't need no voice to dig coal." Bone's father blew smoke in Aunt Mattie's face and headed down the road.

She sputtered something about hopeless cases and strode off in the other direction in a huff.

Bone caught Will by the arm. "Don't pay her any mind." She pulled him toward the door.

Bone couldn't recall when Will had stopped talking. Folks said it was after his daddy got caught in that cave-in back in '33 and died down in the depths of Big Vein. Bone didn't remember, seeing as she was only three at the time. Will couldn't have been more than five. Most folks let Will be. Some thought he was simple. Some joked he didn't have anything to say yet. Bone liked to tell people he had a Gypsy curse cast upon him. Most folks said the acorn didn't fall far from the tree. Will's daddy had been a quiet man, too, they said.

Will held open the screen door as Bone marched into the store, past the old men playing checkers on the cracker barrel, past the RC Colas frosting in the cooler and Red Goose work boots stacked on the shelf, right up to the counter. Uncle Junior and Mr. Price were standing there jawing with Mr. Scott, who ran the commissary.

Bone cleared her voice. "Mr. Scott, Will Kincaid here has himself a job at Big Vein," she announced.

"I got what he needs, Miss Bone." Mr. Scott grinned. He looked Will up and down a bit and then went into the back room. Will shifted from foot to foot while the men hanging about the store slapped him on the back and shook his hand.

"We can use a big, strong 'un like you down there," Mr. McCoy said.

Will stood even taller as Uncle Junior shook his hand. Will was half a head taller than most of the men in the room—except of course Uncle Junior. Both of Mama's brothers were like trees blowing in the wind.

"We take care of our own, Will," Uncle Junior said. He winked at Bone, which made her feel better. Her uncle had been in the mines even longer than her daddy, and he'd look after them both. But she also knew he'd meant something else. Will was only fourteen, but on account of his size and his daddy's death, the mine super had turned a blind eye to Will's age when he scratched sixteen on the form. Everyone in the Big Vein camp knew how old everyone else was, but they also thought Will would never make it through high school or get drafted or even get a job at the powder plant over in Radford. Not without a voice.

"With the war on now, we don't have near enough men to do the job," Mr. McCoy added. The men fell to discussing whether there were enough hands to mine more than one shift this year, like they did before the war.

"We're going to lose more and more as the war goes on." Uncle Junior creased the newspaper and stuck it in his back pocket.

One of the headlines read *Draft Gearing Up*.

Mr. Scott emerged from the back of the store with an armful of goods. He laid the bank clothes and other things out on the counter and said he'd be back directly. He disappeared into the storeroom again. Will swelled up a bit looking at it all. Two pairs of long handle underwear. Bib overalls. Shirt. Overall jacket. Brogan shoes. Miner's cap. A light. A leather belt with a loop on it. A small pickaxe. A whistle. Will pulled the cap on and hefted the pickaxe. He looked like a regular miner.

Bone didn't like the look of him all grown up, even if it meant he could help his mother out. He could put food on the table, he'd written on a little scrap of paper the other night. Bone couldn't argue with that. But she didn't have to like it.

She snatched the cap off his head and put it on hers.

Mr. Scott emerged from the back carrying a battered tin pail.

"Will, this here dinner bucket was your daddy's." Mr. Scott limped around the counter to hand it to Will.

"Scotty and Will Senior were down in shaft twenty-three together that day," Uncle Junior whispered to Bone.

"William would've wanted you to have it when you was ready to go down in the mines," Mr. Scott said. "It was his father's before him."

The bucket had "W. Kincaid" scratched across the lid.

The dinner bucket was like Daddy's and everyone else's. Bone had a vague memory of helping her mother pack Daddy's lunch. Bone would pour water in the bottom compartment, then tamp on the inner lid so Mama could pack biscuits and ham and little jars of jelly or apple butter on top of it. She always packed an extra biscuit or two. Then she set the little tray down on top so she could put a piece of cake or pie on it. While everything was still warm, she clamped the lid down tight.

The bucket carried everything a man needed. That's what Daddy always said. Now Mrs. Price packed his bucket.

Bone reached for the lid, but pulled back quick. Will's father had had the bucket with him when he died.

Bone stepped away from the counter.

"Bone?" Uncle Junior asked her. "You okay?"

She nodded, snapping the mining light onto the cap. She needed a story, and it needed to be a whopper. Bone adjusted the light and grabbed Will's new pickaxe from him. "You heard the one about Jack and the Cyclops?"

Uncle Junior shook his head.

"Jack was trapped in this deep, dark cave with a hungry one-eyed giant." Bone clicked on the light on the miner's cap. "Only the big fella couldn't see real good in the dark of the cave. But he could smell that boy Jack crouching amongst his sheep. So the Cyclops groped his way toward the flock." Bone groped her way past the canned peas and work boots. She crouched down, pickaxe in hand. "Jack leapt up and—*wham*. He stuck his pickaxe plumb in the monster's eyeball."

Uncle Junior and Mr. McCoy laughed.

"Jack ran all the way home," Bone concluded.

Will lifted the pickaxe out of her hands. He tilted his head toward the counter and showed her the few coins he had in his pocket.

Bone knew what he was saying. *This is all I got.*

"Mr. Scott." Bone went up the counter. Leaning across it, still wearing the lamp, she lowered her voice. "Will's a little worried about how he's going to pay for all this."

Mr. Scott and the rest of the men in the store howled.

"Don't you worry none, son," Mr. Scott reassured Will. "It gets taken out of your paycheck. It all does." He proceeded to wrap up everything in brown paper, tying the parcels off with the same string he used for meat orders.

"You belong to the company now," Mr. McCoy called after Will as he hugged the packages to his chest and walked out of the store.

Bone calculated he might belong to the Superior Anthracite Company for quite a while.

After they stepped out on the porch of the commissary, Will's arms loaded down with parcels, Uncle Junior hollered, "Son, you'll want this." He came through the screen door carrying Will's dinner bucket.

Will shifted some packages so he could reach for the pail, but before Bone knew it, Uncle Junior was thrusting the bucket into her hands.

As soon as she laid her fingers on the metal, it all went dark inside her head. She could hear the moaning of timbers giving way and the rumble of rock collapsing around her. Big Vein had swallowed up Will's daddy in black dust and rock. Light and warmth drained out of Bone.

Will grabbed the bucket from her frozen hands, dropping his packages all over the porch.

"Bone, honey, you all right?" asked Uncle Junior. He looked from her to Will and back.

Bone blinked hard and nodded, her jaws clamped down. She couldn't speak, at least until she got that awfulness out of her head.

"Have you been to see your mamaw lately?" her uncle asked with a peculiar look on his face.

Bone scooped up Will's parcels and stacked them back in his arms. She avoided looking him in the eye. He'd told her to go see Mamaw, too, after that first time she'd seen a story. Mamaw could fix most bodily ailments with the right herb. But this wasn't like she had the whooping cough or some such. Bone was seeing things, and she was scared. Maybe it would go away, Bone had told Will back then. Obviously, it hadn't.

Bone pecked her second favorite uncle on the cheek before he could ask any more questions and set off down the road.

She heard the older man slap Will on the back again. "Well, Mr. Kincaid, you best get your gear home. I'll see you down in the mines. Evening, Bone."

She stole a glance in her uncle's direction. He was headed toward the river.

Will caught up to Bone. He set down his packages and the bucket. He tore off a piece of the wrapping paper and scribbled out a note.

He pressed it into her right hand.

Bone shrugged and shoved the note in her pocket without reading it. Then she pulled it out again right quick.

"What the heck?" she exclaimed.

She held up two scraps of paper. A ragged slip of brown butcher paper—the note he'd given her—and a folded piece of cream paper.

She unfolded the other paper and held it taut for him to see. The words were written in black block letters. *THE GIFT KILLED YOUR MOTHER.*

"Did you write this?" Bone measured out her words as carefully as the letters were written. He had slipped notes in her pockets in the past to remind her of things. *Study for the math test. Get more hyssop tea for my mother. Tell your daddy I'd like a job.*

No. Will shook his head hard for good measure.

She knew he didn't. He'd never say anything like this. "What does it mean?"

Will shrugged.

The darkness of the mine pulled at her. And Will, he was standing there, surrounded by all of his gear, ready to follow his daddy down there. And now some so-and-so was trying to tell her that her mama was killed, too. Everyone knew she died of the influenza.

Bone clenched the note in her fist and took off running toward Flat Woods.

And Will let her be.

Bone pelted down the gravel road past rows of little gray clapboard houses, past the boardinghouse, until she came to where there was only the inviting green of the trees that ran along the river. The forest was called Flat Woods because the land was flat, as flat as it got, there by the New River. The deeper you went in Flat Woods the hillier it became as the trees stretched up the side of the mountain past the mines. Folks hunted and trapped up that way. Bone stayed to the flats. It was dark and cool. The thick green leaves overhead let through dapples of sunlight. The woods were quiet except for the distant chugging of a train, the whirring of cicadas, and the barking of dogs up by the mines. The train whistle should blow soon as the Virginian came into camp.

The running warmed her and cleared the unwanted stories from her mind. For now.

Bone slowed to a walk as she came to the foxholes. During the Civil War, some of the local men had dug these holes to hide in. In the mountains, most people thought the War between the States wasn't their fight. During the day, when the Rebel press-gangs were out looking for new recruits, the men would lie in these holes like shallow graves, covered with leaves and branches. At night, they'd go home to tend the crops and animals and see their families.

Bone stretched out in one of the holes. It was barely big enough for her. It must have been quite a squeeze for a full-grown man eighty-some years ago. Above her the trees towered, and the lush green blotted out the sky. Now she could hear the rush of the river. The hole smelled like the last days of summer, of dirt and grass.

Bone uncrumpled the creamy square of paper she'd found in her pocket. The square had been carefully torn from a bigger sheet, leaving a fuzzy edge along one side. It was nice paper, much nicer than the scraps Will used. It was definitely not his chicken scratch. Each letter had been printed like it'd been typed, only bigger. The paper looked familiar, but Bone couldn't quite place it.

THE GIFT KILLED YOUR MOTHER. She read the words over and over again.

What was the Gift? Is that what she felt when she touched things? And how could it have killed her mother?

Bone had seen Mama's obituary many times. Daddy had taped it to the back of a picture he had on his dresser. He said it was hard to believe sometimes that she was gone. Bone liked looking at the picture on the other side, the one of her mother holding her as a baby. Bone sometimes forgot what Mama looked like. Bone was only six at the time, but she remembered Daddy waking her up that night like it was yesterday. He sat on the edge of her bed for the longest time before he could say anything. When he did, he could barely get it out. *Your mother is gone.*

It wasn't Mama's fault, her dying of the flu, yet sometimes Bone couldn't help being mad at her mother for leaving her behind. But then she would feel even worse for feeling that way. It wasn't fair to Mama. So Bone pushed her anger away. Now some sneaky fool coward was stirring it all up with this stupid note. Bone wanted to rip it into little tiny pieces and forget about everything.

She tore one edge and stopped. She couldn't do it. The paper, the story behind it, tugged at her. What did it mean? She needed to know what happened to her mother.

Bone balled up the note in her hand and pounded her fists in the dirt beside her. She let out a yell of frustration. She was answered by the lonesome wail of the Virginian as it wound its way around the river bend.

She lay in the hole and stared up at the green canopy of leaves above her. A breeze rustled through the treetops, revealing chinks of blue sky.

Bone ran her fingers through the dirt beside her. They brushed against something metal and round, a button or a coin. An image washed through her like a current pulling her toward the rapids. Bone saw a man running and heard a shot echo through the woods. She sat straight up in the hole, dropping the coin in the dirt.

The smell of gunpowder lingered in her nostrils.

If this was the Gift, Bone didn't want it.

3

AFTER SUPPER THAT EVENING, Bone turned the coffee cup around the dish towel in her hand, still pondering the note.

Mrs. Price cleared her throat. Four dinner plates, four saucers, and four sets of knives, forks, and spoons sat on the draining board, waiting for Bone. "At this rate, you might as well leave them out for breakfast." Mrs. Price laughed.

Bone didn't say anything.

"Worried about school?" Mrs. Price asked.

Bone shrugged. Mrs. Price ran the boardinghouse Bone and her father lived in for the last six years. As much as she adored Mrs. P., Bone couldn't talk to her about the note. She wasn't even sure who she could talk to about it. Except Will, of course. Daddy didn't like to talk about Mama. Neither did

Uncle Ash. Maybe Will and Junior were right. Bone should talk to Mamaw.

The knock came at the back door, like it did every evening.

"Go ahead. I'll finish up." Mrs. Price smiled a knowing, adult smile.

Bone pushed open the screen door and joined Will on the back steps. He was wearing his new miner's cap. Will handed her one of his scraps of paper, torn from an envelope most likely. He carried all sorts of bits and pieces around in his pockets. Old grocery lists. Butcher paper. Candy wrappers. Any little thing to write on.

Paper.

"Hold on a sec." Bone jumped up and ran back into the kitchen. She grabbed the parcel from the kitchen table and dashed back outside. "I forgot your present."

She shoved it into his hands. She'd wrapped it in the funny papers and tied it with string. Will grinned, and then switched on the miner's light on his cap. He cut the string with a flick of his pocketknife, and the little notebooks spilled out. Bone had made him four small pads of paper out of old composition books. Each was about the size of a pack of cigarettes and had a stub of a pencil tied to it.

"For down in the mines. One will fit in your overalls pocket," Bone explained though she didn't need to.

Still smiling, Will scribbled out something on one of his new pads.

Thanks. They'll come in handy.

He stuffed the extra notepads in his pockets. Then he pointed to the scrap he'd handed her earlier. She'd almost forgotten it was still in her hand.

Bone smoothed it out and read it in the light of the miner's lamp. His chicken scratch was unmistakable.

What did you see when you touched Daddy's dinner bucket?

Bone read it again and then shook her head. She couldn't tell him that, seeing as he was going down in the mine in a few hours. The thought sent a shiver through her, even though the evening was warm and muggy.

That's okay. You answered my question, he wrote on a new notepad.

Bone knew full well what happened to Will's daddy that day in the mine. Will had saved her from seeing more.

He handed her another scrap.

Did you figure out what your note meant?

Bone shook her head again. She heard her own father's voice in her mind. He was always saying that he didn't believe in nothing he couldn't see, taste, hear, or touch. Anything else was superstitious nonsense. But Bone couldn't deny what she saw when she touched certain things.

"Do you think my seeing things in objects is the Gift?" Bone asked.

Will scribbled something out.

Could be. Wasn't your mama a nurse?

"She had some training." Bone wasn't sure what he was getting at. Her mother had taken care of all the people around Big Vein when they were sick, but she'd never finished nursing school. At least that's what Bone remembered. "Why?"

Might be different Gifts. Your Uncle Ash is good with animals.

Bone stared at Will's face in the dim light. He was looking at her like he expected her to put it all together. Sometimes he was quicker to figure out things than she was, and she was feeling a few steps behind.

"What difference does it make that he's good with animals? And how could the Gift kill Mama?"

Will shrugged. *Maybe Mother Reed knows.*

Mother Reed was what folks called Bone's grandmother. They went to her for all sorts of herbs and tinctures. To Bone, though, she was Mamaw. But she did know things.

Bone shrugged.

As she stared out into the yard, she could see the light from his lamp bob up and down. She wasn't entirely sure she wanted to solve this mystery, though. She wanted it to stay summer. Forever.

"Daddy will be mad if you run down your battery before work tomorrow," Bone said, reminded of where he was headed in the morning.

Will flicked the light off, and they sat in comfortable silence, thinking their own uncomfortable thoughts, until Mrs. Price called her in.

"Be sure you bathe, young lady," Mrs. Price told Bone as she trudged up the back steps. "You got school tomorrow."

As if she could forget. "Yes, ma'am."

After a speedy bath in the washroom they all shared, Bone padded through the hall in her pajamas. She paused by her daddy's room. The radio was still playing down in the parlor, the murmur of voices telling her father—and Miss Johnson—the news of the war. Her father had been awfully preoccupied with it, even during dinner. He'd left the radio on despite Mrs. Price's glares.

Bone ducked into her father's room. The picture was where it always was, front and center on his dresser. Mama sat on the porch of their old house holding a toddler. Holding Bone. The happy radiated off the black-and-white photograph. Bone touched the silver frame and felt a chord of sadness—and perhaps something bitterer—mixed in with the happy. She could see Daddy looking at this photo every morning. Yet the happy was stronger than the sad. Bone flipped over the frame and read the obituary taped to the backside. The fading print said that Willow Reed Phillips died on March 16, 1936, from a sudden illness. She was survived by a loving husband and young daughter. Bone wiped a smudge off the glass and placed the frame back on the dresser next to her father's pocket watch and comb and a letter.

It was lying open, and Bone could see the words *Selective Service* across the top. Her stomach dropped as she read the first line. *Greetings. Having presented yourself to a local board . . . you are ordered to report to . . .* The words started to swim on the page. Bone saw the word *Army.* And the date. *September 21, 1942.*

Her daddy had gotten himself drafted.

"Bone?" Her father stood in the doorway packing his pipe with tobacco and watching her. He tamped the tobacco down in the bowl of the pipe over and over again before he spoke. "Let's get you ready for bed." He shooed her into her own room next door.

Neither of them said anything until he pulled back the quilt and motioned her to hop in.

Bone slid under the covers and lay there for half a second. "That letter." She sat up in bed. She wasn't ready to let it go. "I didn't mean to look."

Daddy lit his pipe. "I was going to tell you." He took a deep pull and then let out a wisp of smoke. "I didn't want to ruin your first day of school."

"Do you have to go?" Bone watched the smoke swirl above his head. She'd never thought the war would touch them.

"It's a draft, honey. I have to report in a fortnight."

"Report?" She knew what he meant, but all she could do was repeat his words, hoping they meant something else. "Where?" She had two weeks. Less than that now.

"For the army. I'm hoping I'll get assigned to my old unit, the First Battalion." He sat down next to her. "I think they're in Africa right now. It'll be hot in the desert." He pulled on his pipe as he talked. "But they might be in Italy by the time I get there."

Her father seemed to be relishing the thought of going off to war. And Africa or Italy might be pretty interesting, if it weren't for the Nazis and their tanks. But he shouldn't be happy about going to war—or leaving her.

"Aren't you too old?" Bone asked. He'd already fought one war, and that should be enough. She felt the tears coming.

"Hey there, young lady." Daddy got out his hankie and dabbed her tears away. "Now there's a war on, they're taking men up to the grand old age of forty-five. And I am far from that old."

Bone knew for a fact he was almost that old. He might have lied about his age to join up at the end of the Great War, but that cake Mrs. Price made him in July still had forty-one candles on it. That gave her an idea.

"You lied about your age the first time. You could do it again."

Her father shook his head. "It don't work like that, honey."

"Maybe there's something wrong with you. Uncle Junior got out of the first war on account of his flat feet. I heard a story about this man jumping off his barn to make his arches fall. Or we could hide you in Flat Woods. Whenever the government comes looking—"

"Whoa, Bone, honey." Her father laughed. "I don't want to get out of it. I want to do my duty."

"But . . ." Bone dug deep for some other reason, any reason to make her daddy stay.

"But nothing," he said firmly. "There's some bad people out there who need to be stopped. I don't like leaving you, but I have to do my part."

Bone searched her father's gray-green eyes. He was going, and no amount of talking on her part was going to change that. The fight went right out of her.

She pulled the covers over her head. "You can't leave me, too," she choked out. Her mother was gone. Will was going down in the mines. And now, the worst of the worst, her father was going off to war and maybe to get himself killed. The tears came in earnest. Daddy peeled the covers off her, wrapped his arms around Bone, and let her cry.

When she was cried out, Daddy disappeared for a moment and then returned with a butter-yellow cardigan. Bone recognized it instantly. It had been Mama's.

He pressed it into her hands. "It's yours now, Bone. Your mother would've wanted you to have it."

The sweater tingled against her fingertips. Warmth flooded through Bone like one of Mamaw's teas. She almost dropped the sweater. Instead, she held it to her cheek, shut her eyes, and breathed deep.

She was five or six, and her mama had on this same sweater, the sleeves pushed up to the elbows. Her fingers probed Bone's arm where she'd fallen on it while climbing a tree at Mamaw's. She closed her eyes as if consulting something in her head. "Nothing broken, little monkey. A little ice and one of Mamaw's willow bark tinctures should make it feel all better." Bone could smell the lavender as her mother leaned in close to kiss her forehead.

Not every object told a bad story.

Bone opened her eyes. "Daddy, did Mother have a Gift?"

Something warred across her father's face then. It went from soft and fatherly to sharp and angry and back in a few heartbeats. Daddy finally said, with a catch in his voice, "She had two. One was a gift for people. Sick people. She would have been a wonderful nurse."

"What was the other?" Bone asked. He wasn't getting off the hook that easy.

Her father fought back a smile. "You, silly." He winked. "Your mother left me the best gift of all. She left me you."

Bone couldn't help tearing up a little bit again. "That's not what I meant."

"I know." Her father rose and kissed her on the top of the head. "Now you go to sleep. We both got big days tomorrow." He closed the door gently.

Bone pulled the butter-yellow sweater over her like a blanket. The soft strains of her mother crooning "You Are My Sunshine" lulled her to sleep.

Sometime in the middle of the night, Bone dreamed she was drowning. Unable to catch her breath, she fought through layers of buttery yellow yarn. And when she broke through to the surface, Aunt Mattie's face was peering down at her.

Bone woke in a sweat and pushed the sweater to the floor.

4

IN THE MORNING, Bone crept down the back steps of the boardinghouse. She was wearing her favorite blue flannel shirt and dungarees. As she sat on the bottom step to slip on her boots, she could hear the radio playing in the dining room. More news of battles overseas. Bone was determined not to think about her daddy going off to war. At least not today.

"Where do you think you're going, young lady?" Mrs. Price asked. She stood in the kitchen door, her arms crossed, waiting for Bone. "Your daddy said you were to wear one of your new dresses to school today." Mrs. Price waved her spatula toward the top of the stairs.

Bone stomped back up to her room. Three cotton print dresses that she'd been ignoring since Mrs. Price hemmed them on Sunday hung on the closet door. Her father had made a particular point of Bone dressing like a young lady this last year of school at Big Vein Elementary. Next year, she'd be off to high school in town twenty miles away, and she might as well get used to it now, seeing as the big school had a dress code, her father reasoned. So he'd traded Mrs. Price a couple loads of kindling and a few bags of Mamaw Reed's special woman's tea for several dresses.

Mrs. Price was a wizard with her Singer sewing machine and a hundred-pound feed sack. The boardinghouse owed much of its decor to the King Arthur Flour Company. For as long as Bone could remember, feed and flour sacks were made out of pretty cotton prints that all the ladies used for fabric. That hadn't changed since rationing for the war started back in May. The curtains in Bone's room were made from border sack. It was a special flour or sugar sack with a pretty border just for making curtains or towels. This one was white with morning glories and a blue scalloped edge. The dish towels and valances in the kitchen had big red roses on them courtesy of the Southern Sugar Company. And the doll Mrs. Price had given her when Bone and her daddy first moved into the boardinghouse had been cut out of the preprinted pattern off a sack of salt. That was before Mrs. Price realized Bone didn't have time or patience for dolls.

The dresses hanging in front of her now were made out of the nicer patterns. One was blue and green plaid. Another was pink with white dogwoods on it. The last one was light blue with little daisies. Mrs. Price had draped the butter-yellow cardigan over this one and lined up a pair of saddle shoes and white socks underneath it.

"You'd better shake a tail feather, young lady," Mrs. Price called from the bottom of the stairs.

Bone sighed as loudly as she dared and kicked off her trusty boots, knocking over her stack of *National Geographic*s by the bed. She stripped off her clothes and left them in a pile where she stood. Pulling the light blue dress over her head, she poked her arms through the yellow sweater. It still smelled of lavender and talcum powder, with a hint of mothball. Mama's sweater hung big on Bone's shoulders as she gazed at herself in the mirror.

She looked downright respectable. And maybe even a bit like her mother.

At least I don't match the curtains.

"Bone!"

"Coming!" She slipped on her socks and shoes before dashing down the stairs.

"Much better." Mrs. Price pulled Bone's hair into a ponytail. She handed Bone an egg biscuit wrapped in wax paper and a sack lunch that smelled like fried chicken. "You better hurry. No dillydallying along the way."

Bone raced down the back steps and off across the dusty yard to the road.

The mining camp school was a quarter mile away. Bone ran along the gravel past the Webbs' house and the Linkouses' and a few other weather-beaten company houses. She slowed to a walk as she came to the Alberts' place next to the church. The parsonage always gleamed; from afar, it was a speck of bright white clapboard, brighter than the church even, amongst the dull gray of the company houses. The lace of the front curtain parted for a moment, long enough for Bone to see Aunt Mattie scowl at her, and then it snapped shut again.

The school bell rang, and Bone started running up the road again.

She creaked open the heavy door of the upper-grade class of the two-room school as Miss Johnson was taking roll.

"Pearl Linkous? Opal McCoy? Laurel Phillips?"

"Here." Bone eyed the room.

The fifth and sixth graders stared at her as she made her way toward the back two rows where the seventh graders sat. There were a lot of empty seats there. No Will. He was older than Bone but had been left behind—twice—on account of not speaking. No Bonnie Dillon. She'd moved away when her mother got a job in an ammunition plant. Her father had been killed somewhere in the Pacific.

Still Bone hesitated, not sure where she fit anymore. She'd always sat with Will. Ruby was flanked snugly by Opal and Pearl, and they'd put their bags on the seats around them.

The three of them snickered as Bone stood there at the end of their row.

"Psst." Jake Lilly motioned to a desk in front of him and Clay Whitaker.

Bone gratefully slid into the seat, but not before checking that Jake hadn't kicked the folding seat back up. It was a classic boy move to watch the girl fall on her keister.

"Not this time," Jake whispered. "Wouldn't want to give them little jewels the satisfaction." He nodded toward Ruby and her friends, and the way he said "little jewels" was anything but precious.

"Little Jewels," Bone whispered, more to herself than Jake. "I like that." That nickname just might stick.

Miss Johnson talked about the geography of the war and how they'd be studying England and France and Italy. This time last year Pearl Harbor hadn't happened and the war seemed so far away. Now it was "our fight," as Bone's daddy liked to say.

Miss Johnson started writing out European capitals on the chalkboard. As the chalk scratched across the black slate, Ruby passed notes to Opal and Pearl—and Robert Matthews, the mine operator's son. He was always saying his father was going to send him away to school. Every year Robbie Matthews was right back there in the rows at Big Vein Elementary.

It had been him and the Little Jewels who'd been with Ruby yesterday at the river. Robbie had grabbed Bone's overalls off the tree limb. Bone stared at the back of his pointy head. Did he put the note in her pocket? They'd never said more than two words to each other, at least since she'd thrashed him in first grade for picking on Will. What would Robbie Matthews know about her mother? Not a thing. Bone shook her head and turned her eyes back to the board.

The morning wore on like a sermon on a hot day. Miss Johnson informed the seventh graders that they'd be writing reports on one of the capitals on the board. Bone found her mind wandering to the London of *A Tale of Two Cities*, the Paris of *The Hunchback of Notre Dame*, and the Rome of her *National Geographic*s. And to Will, now of Big Vein. It felt as far away as those cities on the board.

Clay Whitaker poked her awake with a sharpened pencil in time for lunch.

⁓

"Damn, Bone. You look like a girl." Jake grinned as he and Clay plopped into the seats next to her at the picnic table. It was still warm enough for them to eat their sack lunches outside. Jake unwrapped several pieces of fried chicken from a sheet of greasy wax paper. Clay pulled out a couple jelly biscuits from his pockets. Without a word, Jake passed Clay a drumstick.

Bone knew their stories. Clay's father, Chuck, worked down the mines with Daddy—and now Will. The Whitakers had six kids, and all their names started with a C. Jake's father was the outside man at Big Vein. He ran the tipple and worked the machinery. Jake only had two baby sisters. Bone often wondered what it would be like to have even one brother or sister.

Bone smoothed out the wrinkles in her new dress. She had to admit this was a pretty one, with the little flowers all over it.

"Maybe we should call you Bone Meal," said a voice over Bone's shoulder. Ruby stood there in her store-bought Sears and Roebuck dress flanked by Pearl and Opal. The Little Jewels. Bone would have to tell Will that one. "At least that's something useful," Ruby sneered. Pearl and Opal dutifully giggled.

"I'd rather be useful than a Little Jewel," Bone snapped back. The boys laughed.

Bone and Ruby might be cousins, but they'd never been too friendly. Her daddy would make Bone play with Ruby at family gatherings, but it never ended well. Bone pulled down the sleeves of her butter-yellow sweater and breathed in her mother's lavender.

"Well, I'll take Bone's company, whether she was dressed in a feed sack or overalls or a tractor tire, over yours any day." Jake licked the remains of fried chicken from his fingers as he talked.

At that, Ruby glared at Bone and turned on her heel, leading her followers back to their table. Bone could tell this wasn't over by a long shot.

"You know, Bone, you never did tell us that story about them mules and that outhouse." Clay shook a nearly picked clean drumstick in her direction.

A slow smile came to Bone's lips, and she launched into her tale. "There was this boy named Jack. His daddy sent him to borrow a mule from the mean ole man up the road. Folks said he'd cheated a band of Gypsies to get that mule. Those Gypsies warned him she'd be his undoing. The old man laughed and run them off with a shotgun."

A couple of fifth graders, who were always together, lingered by the big tree next to their table, listening. Jake elbowed Clay to make room, which he did grudgingly. Several sixth graders at the next table pretended not to listen.

Bone didn't miss a beat. "Jack knocked on the miser's door and asked real nice to borrow the mule. He even offered to give the old man one of the pups from their best hunting dog. He ran Jack off with his shotgun."

One of the sixth-grade boys bit into an apple with a satisfying crunch. "Shush," a girl whispered as she quietly unwrapped the wax paper around her egg salad sandwich and then handed him half. "Go on, Bone."

"Yeah, what did Jack do?" one of the sixth graders asked.

"Well, Jack hatched a plan to get even. He waited until the old man went to his johnny house. Then he hitched the mule up to it and smacked her on the backside. And sure enough, that mule pulled the outhouse—and its occupant—clear over to the next county."

Bone's audience all laughed. Maybe this year wouldn't be so bad. She shared Mrs. Price's preacher cookies with everyone as Ruby glared at her from the far picnic table. *Not so bad at all.*

5

MISS JOHNSON TUCKED A STRAY PIECE of hair behind her ear and proceeded to scratch a triangle on the chalkboard. She labeled each side and then turned to the class. "If this is a right triangle and side A is two inches and side B is three inches, how long is side C?"

Bone stared at her paper, hoping Miss Johnson wouldn't call on her. Most of the seventh grade did the same. Robbie Matthews was the only one who ever tried to answer the math questions, and he was scribbling away in his composition book.

A voice said dreamily, "3.464 . . ." The voice trailed off. It was Ruby. And she hadn't even written anything down. Ruby usually kept silent in class these days. Now she was studiously avoiding looking at anyone. *It was like she hadn't meant to say the answer out loud.*

Miss Johnson looked pleased. Robbie Matthews did not.

"She didn't raise her hand, Miss Johnson." Robbie had a distinct whine in his voice.

The Little Jewels glared at Ruby, and Jake snickered at some comment Clay had whispered to him.

"Ruby is absolutely right," Miss Johnson said loudly, and the class quieted. "Would you like to share how you arrived at the number, Miss Albert?"

Ruby cringed. She managed to say something about the squares of the sides equaling the square of the long side, all the while clutching something in her right hand.

Robbie muttered, "Lucky guess."

"She did not guess," Bone said a little more loudly than she intended. She wanted to shut Robbie up, not broadcast it to the front row. The fifth and sixth graders were now staring at her.

Ruby whipped around to hush Bone and dropped the thing she'd been clutching. It skidded toward Bone's feet. Ruby was flushed with anger now, but Miss Johnson was showing the class how to solve the equation Ruby had done in her head.

Bone glanced down. The thing was an arrowhead, and she knew exactly where it came from.

❧

They'd found it at the end of July. After her father's birthday dinner, Bone and Ruby had been walking along the river. Daddy had insisted, like always, that they try to get along. Bone had picked up the arrowhead and started to spin a tale about a brave young warrior girl who'd saved her tribe. Started to. When she wrapped her hand around the sharp edges of the stone tip, images roiled through her like a dam bursting. She saw a young native man, not much older than Will, loose the arrow into a buck with a stand of antlers. Pain ripped through her as the deer stumbled and staggered into the water to escape the hunter. The buck was swept out into the current; he struggled for a bit, the fear overwhelming the pain in Bone's head. She could feel herself being pulled under, too. And then the buck's head dipped below the water.

"The deer drowned," Bone gasped. She dropped the arrowhead and backed away from it.

"What in the Sam Hill are you babbling about?"

"The story was in—" Bone pointed at the arrowhead lying between them. "It."

She told Ruby what she'd seen. Bone had had vague hunches about things when she touched some objects, like the time she just knew a school book had belonged to Mama. That was nothing like this.

Bone had felt the deer die.

She'd shivered, even though it was about a hundred degrees out.

Ruby stared at her peculiarly for another moment and then stooped to pick up the arrowhead herself. She turned it over in her palm, squeezing the arrowhead tight in her hand. She closed her eyes even tighter, like she was concentrating real hard. *Could Ruby see the story, too?* Bone held her breath as she watched her cousin's face.

After a second or two, her eyes opened—and then narrowed into slits as she glared at Bone. Ruby stood up straight. "You're such a liar, Bone Phillips," she practically spat the words in Bone's face.

She took a step back. "Am not!" She'd seen what she'd seen. She didn't know why, but she'd seen it.

"Then you must be crazy! There's nothing in this stupid rock." Ruby shoved it in her pocket, turned on her heel, and marched back toward the boardinghouse.

Ruby slammed the front door, leaving Bone standing alone in the yard, her thoughts and fears swirling around her, fixing to drown her. *Was she crazy? Was she seeing ghosts? Daddy would say that was superstitious nonsense. Would anybody believe her?* Seeing as crazy folks got sent to lunatic asylums, Bone decided then and there she best keep the stories she saw in objects to herself—or at least to just herself and Will.

◦—◦

A still-pink Ruby searched the floor for her arrowhead, until she locked eyes with Bone.

"Well, hand it to me, Bone Meal." Ruby jabbed a finger toward the stone at Bone's feet.

Bone couldn't quite reach it with her foot, so she reluctantly picked up the charm off the wooden floor, holding the stone's still-sharp edges between her fingers. She braced herself for the flood of images, expecting to see the deer drown all over again. This time, Aunt Mattie's voice rang in her head, yelling awful things at Ruby. *You'll never amount to anything. What man will have you looking like that? You are a constant disappointment to me.* Ruby was squeezing the arrowhead in her palm until its edges drew blood. The sting blotted out the rest of the world, including her mother's tongue-lashing.

As Bone opened her eyes, she was painfully aware of her cousin's horrified stare.

"What did you see? Me?" Ruby asked. "Don't say a thing."

Bone narrowed her eyes at her cousin. *Ruby had believed her all along.*

"Miss Albert. Is there anything you and Miss Phillips want to share with the class?"

"No ma'am." Ruby's face reddened again as she turned around, but Bone saw the look of anger and something else in her eyes. Bone stashed the arrowhead in her math book.

Ruby wouldn't even look in Bone's direction for the rest of class, and Bone didn't much care if she did.

After school, Bone waited for Ruby by the picnic tables. The boys were tossing a ball back and forth in the yard. No one liked to rush right home. Home meant chores for most.

"Give it," Ruby demanded as she stuck her hand in Bone's face. "Quick, before they see." But it was too late. Robbie Matthews, Pearl, and Opal had spotted them.

"Are you coming, Ruby?" Robbie asked. He was carrying her books. That only happened in the movies.

"Just as soon as Bone Meal gives me back my property," Ruby said.

Bone opened up her math book to the spot where she'd stashed the arrowhead. She held up the book like a platter.

"Why do you want that old thing?" Opal asked. Pearl cackled.

Ruby flushed. "I don't." She snatched the arrowhead and flung it off in the woods. Or at least that was her intention. The arrowhead smacked Clay Whitaker on the ear.

Robbie Matthews had a good laugh at that.

Ruby leaned in close to a stunned Bone and whispered, "Be careful. Mama says the Gifts are the devil's work."

Ruby knew about the Gifts. That day at the river, Ruby, of course, had been the one who'd picked up Bone's overalls and hung them back on the bush.

"*You* put the note in my pocket!" Bone whispered back, a little louder than she intended.

Ruby pressed a finger to her lips and whipped around, the Little Jewels nipping at her heels.

Bone couldn't move. She just stared dumbly after Ruby and her friends strolling toward the Matthews' big house on the hill.

"What in tarnation was that about?" Clay asked, still holding his earlobe where the arrowhead had struck him.

Bone wasn't entirely sure.

"You all want this?" Jake was wiping off the bloodied arrowhead with his handkerchief.

Bone carefully took the object, hankie and all, from Jake. It tingled a bit, even through the fabric. Bone wrapped the arrowhead up tight and stuffed it in her pocket.

The boys offered to walk her home, but Bone wanted to be by herself. She was at a loss.

Why would Ruby put that note in her pocket? She'd seen a glimpse of how Aunt Mattie treated Ruby. *What did she know about the Gift?*

6

RUBY'S WORDS STILL RUNG in Bone's ears as she dashed up the boardinghouse steps. Bone shut the screen door with an unsatisfying thwack and slammed her composition book on the small kitchen table. She stuffed the arrowhead wrapped in Jake's kerchief deep in her sweater pocket.

"Rough day at school?" Mrs. Price chopped greens on the butcher block. She didn't look up.

Bone sank onto the stepstool by the icebox. "School ain't . . . isn't the problem."

"Ruby?"

Bone's head snapped up. Mrs. Lydia Price knew everything that went on around Big Vein, above or below. And she and Bone's mother had been friends since they were little.

Mrs. Price threw handfuls of greens into the pot of boiling water on the stove until it was full to the brim, the smell of the ham bone already rising in the steam.

"What killed Mama?" Bone asked. She really wanted to know why she'd died at all, but that question didn't have an answer.

Mrs. Price turned to Bone, a fistful of greens still in hand. "What did Ruby say to you?"

Bone couldn't tell Mrs. Price exactly what had been said. The Gift might be a family thing. And Mrs. Price wasn't family, not really. "Nothing."

"I swear that Ruby is getting to be just like her mother." Mrs. Price dropped the last of the greens in the pot. "You know your mother died of the influenza."

Bone nodded. That was the sudden illness in the obituary.

"Your daddy's parents died of it, too, after the Great War."

Bone rubbed the sleeve of the yellow sweater between her fingers. She caught a whiff of lavender. Then a flash of warmth, like fever, washed over her. Bone scrambled to peel off the sweater.

"What did Ruby say?" Mrs. Price eyed Bone.

"Nothing." Bone sank back onto the stool.

"Your mother and Mattie were a lot like you and Ruby." Mrs. P. wiped her hands on her King Arthur Flour apron. "Except they started out close, but then Mattie changed."

"How did she change?" Bone sat up.

"Sometimes folks, even sisters, grow in different directions." With a shrug, Mrs. Price stirred the greens once, put the lid on, and turned down the heat a mite.

"But how?" Bone wasn't going to let Mrs. Price off the hook so easy.

"Well, your mother was more of a free spirit." Mrs. Price waved the wooden spoon in Bone's general direction. "She ran around the countryside with her brother Ash and helped your grandmother with her work. Mattie was more concerned about socials and dressing nice."

Like Bone and Ruby.

"And Mattie started going to church two, three times a week," Mrs. Price added. She cracked open the oven, and Bone spied an extra-large pan of chicken and dumplings on one rack and corn bread on another. Mrs. P. poked the pan of corn bread with a toothpick before closing the oven door. It was more food than they usually had for weekday supper. Plus a pie was cooling on the windowsill above the sink.

"Are we having a visitor?" Bone sprang to her feet. "Who?"

Mrs. Price nodded. "Thought that would cheer you up."

It did. Bone set the table happily. They hadn't had a visitor at the boardinghouse since the war began. Before Pearl Harbor, back when the Depression was on, men (and boys) used to ride the rails looking for work. At least once a month, a man from Pennsylvania or New York or Ohio would step off the freight car and walk down the road to the mine office to ask about work. The jobs were nearly always taken, but her daddy would invite the gentleman back to the boardinghouse for one square meal before sending him on his way. The price was telling his story over ham and green beans and apple pie. Bone loved hearing those stories, even if they always had the same sad plot. The bank had taken the farm or the factory had shut down and they heard there was work in the mines or at the powder plant over in Radford. Or they had a mind to work their way south to pick tobacco or apples or even oranges down in Florida.

Now that the war was on everyone seemed to have plenty of work, and the train only brought empty cars thirsty for coal to Big Vein.

As Bone set out the extra plate at the far end of the table, the news of the war—along with the scent of cherry-soaked tobacco—filtered in from the front parlor. Newly scrubbed from the change house, Daddy sat in there smoking his pipe and reading the paper in the big leather chair next to the radio. He liked to smoke one pipe and catch up on the outside world after a long day deep in the mines. It reminded him there was more to the world than Big Vein, he liked to say.

･ ＊ ･

The visitor turned out not to be a dusty, travel-worn man off the train or Uncle Ash or even a Gypsy. Miss Johnson—the only other boarder—entered the dining room arm in arm with a willowy woman in neatly pressed charcoal trousers and a pale blue blouse with padded shoulders—and bright red lipstick. She looked smart and practical and womanly all at once. She reminded Bone of Katharine Hepburn in *Woman of the Year*, the movie they'd showed at the camp earlier this summer. Hepburn played a reporter who traveled the world, but her husband didn't like it much. Bone had made Will sit through both showings of the movie while she imagined she was like Katharine Hepburn. Bone didn't like the ending, but she changed it in her head. She had Hepburn fly off to Spain or England or some such place— instead of staying home with Spencer Tracy.

"Bone, this is Miss India Spencer," Miss Johnson introduced her. "She was my history professor at the women's college in Roanoke."

Bone couldn't recall meeting a woman Miss Spencer's age who wasn't a missus. She had to be as old as Mrs. Price, who was a widow with grown daughters.

"I've heard a lot about you, Bone." Miss Spencer favored Bone with a knowing glance, which made her feel both thrilled and uncomfortable. Bone gulped down her sweet tea.

"Me?" Bone asked. What was there to hear about her?

"Miss Johnson says you know about every story there is to know." The woman had a Yankee accent Bone couldn't place, but she decided it was like Katharine Hepburn's. "I collect stories."

As Mrs. Price ushered everyone into the dining room, India Spencer explained she was part of a government program—the

Virginia Writers' Project—that was collecting folktales from all over the state. The project was part of President Roosevelt's Works Progress Administration, or WPA. Miss Spencer was interested in the stories from the mountains.

"We're making one last effort before the war takes everyone away." She raised a forkful of greens to her mouth. "These are excellent, Mrs. Price."

Mrs. Price beamed as she passed the corn bread.

"Money could be spent better elsewhere. Like the war effort," Daddy said.

"The WPA created a lot of jobs for folks where it was needed, including writers." Miss Johnson jumped to her teacher's defense.

"It's okay. Mr. Phillips is right. The money now is going toward the war. A few of us are volunteering to finish up what we started. We don't want to lose our history. A lot of stories, experience, and wisdom might vanish if folks don't collect them."

Daddy nodded and quickly tucked into his chicken and dumplings.

"Bone, we thought you might like to help Miss Spencer," Miss Johnson said, passing the greens. "You could tell her some of the stories you've heard and maybe take her around to meet people, if that's all right with your father."

Bone looked at Daddy expectantly. She couldn't think of anything else she'd like to do better. "Please, can I? I promise to do my chores and my homework, too."

Her father tried to look stern, like he did when he scolded her, which wasn't often, but Bone only saw that glimmer in his eye when she knew he was bluffing. Daddy winked. "Of course, you can, Laurel. It'll keep you out of trouble. And you might learn a thing or two from Miss Spencer about college and such." He exchanged a look with Miss Johnson, and Bone figured her daddy may have been in on this arrangement from the beginning. "But I want you to stay on this side of the river," he added, pointing his butter knife at her.

"But—," Bone began. If she couldn't cross the river, Bone couldn't go see her grandmother. She didn't like to come to Big Vein much.

"No buts, young lady. That's my condition."

Bone was flabbergasted. He'd never forbidden her to cross the river. He'd never forbidden her to do anything before. She studied her father as he slathered a last biscuit with butter. More and more Daddy was taking Aunt Mattie's side of the family feud. It wasn't really a feud, as far as Bone could tell. Aunt Mattie seemed to be the only one fighting, and it wasn't entirely clear to Bone why. Daddy had once told her that there was a division between the Reed siblings that had only been made worse by her mother's passing. The oldest—Uncle Junior and Aunt Mattie—were the practical ones. The youngest—Bone's mother and Uncle Ash—were the different ones. But all that didn't explain the rift between Aunt Mattie and her own mother, Bone's mamaw. And now her daddy didn't want her to go see Mamaw. It didn't make a lick of sense.

"It's settled then," Miss Spencer said. "Now how about one of those stories?"

Mrs. Price excused herself to get the coffee and pie.

"Oh, now you've done it." Bone's father chuckled as he leaned back in his chair to pack his pipe.

Bone didn't quite know where to start; there were so many stories running through her head, but most of the old-timey ones started this way: "There was this ole boy named Jack . . ." So she told Miss Spencer one of her favorites, the one about Jack and the robbers.

It came to Bone while she was telling the story. Will was right. She needed to talk to Mamaw even if she had to walk the whole five miles to Dry Branch. She would know about the Gifts. When her father left the room, she whispered to Miss Spencer, "My grandmother and Uncle Ash know a ton of stories better than this one."

It wasn't a lie. And Miss Spencer was hooked.

7

THE RAP CAME AT THE SCREEN DOOR as Bone pored over the new *National Geographic* Miss Johnson had given her. She and Miss Spencer were catching up on old times in the parlor. Daddy was glued to the war news again. Bone knew Will'd come. She had a mason jar full of sweet tea ready for him.

Will sat himself on the steps staring off into the darkness beyond the boardinghouse's backyard. Miss Johnson's tabby, Hester Prynne, rubbed up against his shin while he scratched behind the cat's ear. Animals loved Will. Cats. Dogs. Horses. Even baby calves. All seemed attracted to his quiet. The only sounds were the whirring of cicadas, the low voices of the women in the parlor, and the contented purring at Will's feet.

"How was the first day?" Bone sank down beside Will (and Hester) on the wooden step.

In reply, he drank the sweet tea in one long, thirsty gulp.

The Virginian's whistle sounded in the distance. Eight fifteen. The coal train was making its way toward Richmond.

"What was it like down there? In the mine?" Bone asked. "Was it awful?" She asked the last in a whisper.

Will shook his head vigorously.

Your daddy had me digging right off, he wrote out.

"I thought you'd start out hand loading." Bone shivered a bit. Her daddy had told her that the boys worked mostly on filling up the cars or sorting coal up top.

Your daddy said I'm a natural miner.

"He did, huh?" Bone was peeved at both of them. What if something happened to all of them? Daddy, Junior, and now Will?

Linkous twins got stuck hand loading.

Marvin and Garvin Linkous were two years older than Will.

"They are a mite puny," Bone allowed. She was still peeved. "Weren't you scared?"

Will took off his miner's cap and pressed it into Bone's hand. A darkness, a different one, crept over them. She felt fear, mixed with a downright thrill, go through Will as the mantrip plunged into the pitch black of the mine. The 'trip was the squat little train that carried the men to and from the surface. The temperature dropped, and Bone soon heard the sound of digging. She didn't feel scared anymore, though. She felt the peacefulness of it—and a quiet satisfaction. It was what Will felt down there. He could hear himself think, and he was good at it.

Now I can take care of Mama, Will wrote.

Bone nodded and put the cap back on Will's head. His mother had scrubbed floors for the mine superintendent's family ever since his daddy died.

Will handed her another scrap of paper.

How was school? He looked at her expectantly.

"It was Ruby who left the note," Bone finally said. She didn't feel like talking about her daddy going off to war. Or the bad dream she had. She could still see Mattie peering down at her—or was it her mother?—with the yellow sweater between them.

Will raised an eyebrow at her again.

Bone shrugged. She told him about the arrowhead and about what Ruby'd said after school. *Be careful. Mama says the Gifts are the devil's work.*

What are you going to do? Will scratched out.

"Let's take Miss Spencer to see Mamaw after church Sunday."

Will looked at her blankly.

So she explained who Miss Spencer was and how she was collecting stories for the government.

Bone sighed. "I wish it would stay summer." In a forever summer, no one would have to do homework. No one would have to solve mysteries. No one would have to go down in the mines. No one would go off to war.

Will nodded as he stared off into the dark, thinking thoughts she couldn't hear. Then he squeezed her hand before releasing it. He stood, shook out the last drops of tea from the jar, and stepped down into the darkness.

He marched off toward the trees at the edge of the property, toward a twinkling of light in the high grass.

Summer wasn't gone quite yet.

Seconds later Will returned, his hand over the top of the jar, with a lightning bug flashing out its Morse code to the world.

He'd caught the last of summer in a jar for her.

Bone carefully replaced his hand with her own as he gave it to her. Will strode off into the darkness toward his house.

Bone covered the jar with wax paper, which she held in place with a rubber band, and then poked holes in the paper with a toothpick. Throughout the night, tiny flashes of yellow-green light played across her ceiling while she dreamt of floating in the warm waters of the New River on a hot sunny day.

In the morning, the lightning bug was still, and Bone pulled on her blue and green plaid dress and trudged off to school.

8

AFTER CHURCH, Bone wouldn't sit still. Will lounged on the boardinghouse steps like he hadn't seen the sun in a month of Sundays. Bone popped up every five minutes to see if Uncle Ash was coming already. They were waiting for Miss Spencer to change out of her church clothes. Will got out his notebook and scribbled, *He'll get here when he gets here*. Uncle Ash did run on his own time.

"I'm worried Daddy will *get here* before Uncle Ash," Bone confessed.

Will raised an eyebrow at her.

She plopped down beside him. "I arranged for Uncle Junior to take Daddy fishing this morning." Uncle Junior hadn't been as hard to convince as Bone had imagined.

Will scribbled out one word: *Why?*

Bone didn't even look at the paper. "Because," Bone began slowly, "Daddy said not to take Miss Spencer across the river."

Will held up the question again.

Bone shrugged. "I got no idea. He's always let me visit over there whenever I wanted." It was another mystery she wasn't sure she wanted to solve.

The screen door creaked open, and Miss Spencer emerged with a small tan knapsack slung over one shoulder. "Is it far?" she asked.

"It's a fair piece." Bone slathered on a folksy accent for Miss Spencer. "I expect Uncle Ash will be here directly." She popped up again to check the road.

Will leaned back against the twenty-pound sack of coffee they were taking to Mamaw and closed his eyes.

Earlier, Bone had so many questions she wanted to ask Miss Spencer about her work, but none would come to mind now. All Bone could think about was the Gift—and her daddy coming up the road.

The putter of an engine and the crunch of tires on gravel put Bone out of her misery. Her first favorite uncle and his familiar pale yellow pickup were coming toward them. She didn't have to see the back to know it was filled with dogs.

And sure enough, a few minutes later, the yellow truck pulled up beside them on the grass. Uncle Ash's fox terrier, Corolla, hung her head out the driver's-side window, and Kiawah and Kitty Hawk stood with their front paws on the side rails of the truck bed, their tails thunking against the metal. Uncle Ash named his dogs after the places he'd found them.

"Ya'll need a lift?" he asked in his easy way. He crushed a cigarette on his side mirror and put it in his shirt pocket. Then he shooed the fox terrier off his lap, as he stepped out of the cab of the '28 Chevy that had seen many better days.

Uncle Ash shook Will's hand, as he always did, and jerked a thumb toward the back of the truck.

Bone hugged her first favorite uncle. His flannel shirt smelled of peppermint sticks, Lucky Strikes, and dog. Not a bad combination. "I thought you'd never get here." She slid onto the faded bench seat of the Chevy.

The fox terrier skittered up after her.

"Corolla, back of the truck, girl," Ash commanded as he held the passenger door open for Miss Spencer. The dog dutifully hopped out and up into the bed of the truck, where she proceeded to make herself at home in Will's lap. "I'm Ash Reed, by the way, and you must be Miss Spencer."

"Come on," Bone urged, peering down the road.

"Hold your water, Bone." Uncle Ash lit another Lucky Strike and eased into the driver's seat. "Junior took Bay all the way up to Parrott to fish. Your daddy won't see us coming or going." He whispered the last part.

Will always said Ash reminded him of some weary Civil War general after the fighting was all said and done. Uncle Ash was tall and thin, like most of the Reeds. His salt-and-pepper beard was neatly trimmed, and he wore his hair longer than most men in Big Vein. They were all clean-shaven, and their hair was slicked back with a dab of Brylcreem come Saturday night. And Uncle Ash got this faraway look in his eyes sometimes like he was listening for cannon roar.

He slid the rear window open and told Will and the dogs to hold on. He whipped the truck around on the gravel road and headed back toward the river.

"So how's my Forever Girl today?" Uncle Ash finally asked.

"Forever Girl? There's got to be a tale that goes with a name like that," Miss Spencer told him.

Bone loved this nickname—and the story that went with it.

"Care to do the honors, niece?" Uncle Ash asked.

Bone didn't need to be asked twice. "Forever *Boy* was this young Cherokee feller who refused to grow up," she began. "He wanted to wander the woods and play games. Finally his mother laid down the law. He had to work the fields and hunt, get married, and take care of his family. His mother was going to send him to live with his uncle, who would teach him everything he needed to know to be a man."

Miss Spencer got out her pad and pen from her satchel.

"Did you know the Cherokees were a matriarchy?" Bone asked her. "So a man's heirs were his sister's children, not his own."

Miss Spencer admitted she didn't know that.

Uncle Ash laughed. "In case it wasn't clear, Bone is my sister's child."

"Oh, I got that." Miss Spencer smiled.

"Well, old Forever Boy couldn't stomach settling down," Bone continued loudly. "So he decided to run off on his own. However, he was soon lost and starving out in the woods. The Little People found him and invited Forever Boy to live with them. So he never did have to grow up at all."

"Little People?" Miss Spencer asked.

"The Cherokee called them Nunnehi. The Catawba and other tribes have another name for them. I forget," Uncle Ash answered. The truck slowed to a stop at the ferry landing on the river.

"The Little People were here long before any big people," Bone added. "Forever Boy is probably still out there—"

"We're crossing the river on that?" Miss Spencer interrupted, incredulous.

Ash Reed chuckled. "Y'all get out and tie 'er up."

Will hopped down from the bed of the truck, followed by the dogs. Bone scrambled out to help. Mr. Goodwin, the ferryman, had seen them coming down the road and had started across the river toward them. The ferry was no more than a floating platform pulled across the river by a winch. Goodwin's ferry was big enough for one car or a horse and wagon. Larger loads, like delivery trucks, needed to drive down ten miles or so to a bridge to cross. Most folks rode the ferry and walked to wherever they were going.

Miss Spencer eyed the bobbing platform dubiously as it pulled into the little dock. "I see why your grandmother doesn't like to cross the river."

Mr. Goodwin snorted and exchanged a look with Bone. "It's not my ferry that Mother Reed don't like." He threw her a bowline.

"Hey, Mr. Goodwin." Bone wrapped the line around the post and jumped the small gap between the dock and ferry.

Will did the same with the other line. Uncle Ash threw the truck in gear and inched the old Chevy onto the moving platform. Once the truck was on, Will unwrapped the ropes and threw them back to Mr. Goodwin. Will stepped easily over the now larger gap between the dock and ferry, followed by the dogs. Miss Spencer still stood feet planted firmly on the dock until Will reached his hand across to help her on board.

Mr. Goodwin flipped the switch on the winch motor, and the ferry jerked into motion toward the Dry Branch side of the river.

The deck of the tiny ferry bobbed gently under their feet as it was pulled across the current.

"Uncle Ash?"

"Hmm?" he answered, tearing himself away from telling Miss Spencer about the two sides.

"Do you think Forever Boy was wrong to run off to live with the Little People?"

Uncle Ash took a long drag on his cigarette before answering. "I think ole Forever Boy needed to at least try living among the Big People for a spell before he escaped to the woods."

Mr. Goodwin spat his chaw over the side of the rail.

Bone wasn't entirely convinced by Uncle Ash's answer, but it did seem like a fair one. Still, she'd have done the same as Forever Boy.

Soon the ferry ground to a stop on the Dry Branch side, and Mr. Goodwin handed Will the bowline again.

Once on shore, Miss Spencer stopped to look back across the New River at the coal camp carved into the hollow. Bone tried to look with Miss Spencer's eyes. Dingy white houses crowded together along the road going up the hill to the mine. And at the top a black gash of coal spilled out of the earth among some even dingier-looking buildings.

The yellow truck crawled off the ferry, and everyone, dogs and people both, piled back into the Chevy. The harmonies and mandolin pickings of "Unclouded Day" filled the cab of the truck:

". . . where no storm clouds rise
Oh they tell me of an unclouded day . . ."

"Peppermint?" Uncle Ash asked, handing one to Bone. "Will?" He passed one over his shoulder and through the window. "Do not let Corolla have any," he added. "She'll gorge herself like a tick if you let her."

Uncle Ash turned the music down to a low burble.

"Bone, why do you think Forever Boy chose to live with the Little People?" he asked, earnestly.

Miss Spencer was scratching away in her notebook, no doubt writing down the exploits of Forever Boy and the Little People.

"Maybe he was afraid of things changing," Bone finally said.

"Aw, Forever Girl." Uncle Ash put his arm around her. "That's just part of growing up."

That's exactly what Forever Boy was afraid of. Things change. People leave. All when everything was perfectly good before. Almost everything.

9

THE LITTLE YELLOW TRUCK strained up the windy road, a wall of Virginia Pines on either side. Uncle Ash crooned along with the radio while Bone and Miss Spencer harmonized. Miss Spencer stopped singing as the truck passed over the little stone bridge and into sunlight of the clearing that was the Reed "yard."

Uncle Ash elbowed Bone as he slowed the truck down to a crawl.

"It's like *The Secret Garden*," Miss Spencer said softly. "Or *Swiss Family Robinson*."

On one side of the gravel road bloomed a field of flowers and, on the other, herbs and winter vegetables, like dark leafy kale, greened the earth. A stone path cut through the flowers to a small cabin. At one time several families of Reeds and Phillips lived on this land, but most moved down to the mine years ago. This was the only cabin left.

"What a sweet little cottage," Miss Spencer said.

"Oh, that's Mama's office," Ash replied as he drove past it. "We live up there." He pointed to the grove of oaks at the top of the hill.

Miss Spencer peered through the windshield at the trees for a moment. She stole a glance at Ash, and then stuck her head out the truck window, not unlike one of Uncle Ash's dogs, and gawped at the five enormous oak trees they were approaching.

"That's . . ." She ducked her head in the window.

Bone and Ash laughed. He turned off the engine, and the dogs piled out of the truck as it gave one last shudder.

"I think the word you're searching for is—," Ash began.

"Impressive," Miss Spencer interrupted him.

"I was going to say tree house," Ash replied. He put out another cigarette on the mirror before climbing out of the cab.

The Reed house hung between four ancient trees. The fifth one served more to block the view of the house from the road. A curved sloping walkway took you up in the air ten or twelve feet to a porch that wrapped around the house. Everything was held in place by timber and stone columns cleverly hid among the trees. And a stone chimney made from river rock anchored the far side of the house to the earth. To Bone, it'd always looked like a giant hand had set the house down between the trees.

"Ash!" A man came running from the dark green truck parked by the small springhouse around the back of the house. He was a Harless from down Parrott way. "It's Ellie. She's bad."

Uncle Ash sprinted over to the bed of the man's truck, with Bone and Will on his heels. In the back, Mamaw sat in her usual crisp white shirt and trousers, holding the head of a large bloodhound in her lap. The dog was breathing heavy and whimpering as it lay there.

Mamaw stroked the dog's ear. "Ash is here, Ellie. He'll see what's wrong."

Uncle Ash didn't waste any time. He eased himself up into the truck bed and ran his hand over the dog's chest and belly. He closed his eyes and concentrated for a moment. Bone had seen him do this many times before. He was counting breaths or taking a pulse or considering what to do. Bone wasn't exactly sure which. His eyes flashed open. "She's got the bloat, Pete. But her stomach ain't twisted yet."

"Can you save her?" the man asked.

"We'll give 'er a try." Ash jumped down from the tailgate. "Mother, have you got some of that rubber tubing left from your, um, medicinal brewing?"

"Yes, there should be some hanging by the sink down yonder." Mamaw pointed toward her cabin.

"Bone, go fetch a long piece of hose and a bucket. Will, you help Mother and me move Ellie." Uncle Ash rolled up his sleeves as he barked out orders. Only at times like this could Bone imagine he was once an army sergeant.

"What can I do?" Miss Spencer asked.

Bone raced down the stone path through the herb garden to the little cabin where her grandmother prepared her healing potions and tinctures. She inhaled the scent of rosemary and sage as she ran. Inside the back door was a little kitchen that looked more like a mad scientist's lab in the movies. Or maybe a moonshiner's. Jars and vials dried in the sink. The cabinets were filled with dried herbs, powders, and concoctions, neatly arranged and labeled. An intricate setup of flasks and bottles and copper vessels sat on the counter, all connected with rubber tubing. And, sure enough, several lengths of the same rubber hoses hung over the sink. Bone grabbed the longest one, ran out the door, and then shot back in for the bucket that was under the sink.

When she got up the hill, Uncle Ash had moved the ailing dog so that her head hung over the tailgate of the truck. Will and Miss Spencer held the dog while the owner paced back and forth. Uncle Ash took the tubing from Bone and cut a piece of it the length of the dog. Mamaw disappeared into the springhouse with the bucket.

Uncle Ash handed Bone one end of the hose. "Keep it level with the dog's mouth—and away from your feet."

He gently threaded the tube into the dog's mouth. Ellie was so far gone that she barely even whimpered as Ash worked the tube down her throat.

"Uncle Ash, what's this supposed to do?" Bone fed her uncle more tubing as he guided it toward Ellie's stomach.

"You'll see. I hope." Ash stroked the dog's belly. "Okay, this is the last little bit. Better stand clear, Bone."

The warning came about two seconds too late. A mighty belch of air erupted from the dog's mouth. Water and bits of food poured out and around the tube, splashing both Bone's and Ash's boots. And it kept coming. Ellie had had a huge breakfast.

Ash flushed out Ellie's stomach with water. By then the dog was fighting it, and Mr. Harless jumped in to hold her still.

"Always a good sign." Ash grinned at the relieved owner.

Soon Ellie the bloodhound was sleeping comfortably— thanks to one of Mamaw's drafts—in the back of Mr. Harless's truck. Uncle Ash told him not to feed Ellie for a day or so and to get her to the vet in Radford as soon as he could, but she should be all right. Mr. Harless promised to replace the carburetor in Ash's truck and see what other work it needed. And to get Mamaw some new hoses next time he was at the hardware store.

Ash rinsed his boots off under the pump and motioned for Bone to do the same.

"That was quite . . ." Miss Spencer trailed off again.

Mr. Harless's truck bounced gently down the road.

"Impressive?" Ash supplied, with a grin. He lit another cigarette.

Miss Spencer laughed in spite of herself. "Where did you learn to do that?" she asked.

"Oh, Uncle Ash just has a way with animals," Bone replied automatically as she stuck the kibble-encrusted toe of her left boot under the stream of water. It's what she usually said when folks asked about how her uncle, who had no formal schooling whatsoever, knew what was wrong with any animal. Bone stopped as she felt her uncle and grandmother looking at her. Miss Spencer was busy washing her hands.

"Bone, honey, why don't you help me down in my office?" Mamaw asked. It wasn't really a question. "Ash and Will can show Miss Spencer around, and then we'll have some cake."

Ash was leading Miss Spencer back to the house as they shared a cigarette. And Mamaw was already halfway to the cabin. She did not dally. Bone had no trouble imagining Acacia Reed in the army. In another life, perhaps.

Will gave Bone one of his meaningful looks.

This was Bone's chance to ask Mamaw about her mother and the Gift.

10

THIS TIME, Bone breathed in the scents of the herb garden more deeply. Among the rosemary and sage, she could detect hints of mint and lavender and damp earth and green grass, all the smells that reminded her of her grandmother—and her mother. Her mama, with Bone at her side, had spent many long summer afternoons helping Mamaw plant and weed and pick the herbs. They even helped her collect wild medicinals and mosses from the woods around the house. And during the winter, Mamaw tended her plants in the little greenhouse one of her customers had built for her years ago out of old windows.

Mamaw had a way with plants like Uncle Ash had a way with animals. Or so folks said, and Bone had always believed that. But now, as she'd been watching Ash touch that dog, it struck her as familiar. It looked awful much like he'd closed his eyes and could see what was wrong. Bone stopped dead amidst the drying coneflowers on the back porch. He saw something in the animal—like she did in ordinary objects.

Bone pushed the screen door open slowly, feeling a little dizzy from the revelation. Was this the Gift? Was this what Will meant about there being different ones?

Inside Mamaw had set a pot of water on the woodstove and was chucking a small log into its belly. Bone rinsed out the rubber hoses and placed them in the water without Mamaw saying a word. They needed to be "de-dogified" so Mamaw could use them to distill the essential oils she sold or bartered with folks. Or perhaps irrigate the plants in the greenhouse. Someone had built a clever little machine that pumped water from the springhouse to the greenhouse.

Mamaw cleared a spot at the table and shooed Sassafras, one of her favorite calicoes, off her chair. Like her children, she named them all after the plants she loved. "Help me clean these burdock for a minute, Bone." In the center of the table was a wooden bowl of the long brown roots with the green tops still on them.

"You know Ash isn't just good with animals, don't you?" Mamaw asked finally.

She did now. Bone nodded as she plucked the sticky heart-shaped leaves from the useful part of the plant. She set the roots back in the bowl for Mamaw to peel.

Mamaw closed her eyes and wrapped her fingers around a slender root in her hand. "This plant can clean out the blood, reduce swelling, thin a cough, strengthen the liver, and soothe the bowels. You know how I know that?" Her grandmother peeked an eye open at Bone.

"Your mother taught you?" Bone knew there was more to it than that. Great-grandma Daisy had been good with plants, too, but nowhere near as good as her daughter.

"She did. A person can certainly know things without it being their *Gift*." She put a special emphasis on that last word.

"What do you mean by Gift exactly?" Bone asked. Lots of people talked about gifts, like having a gift for throwing a baseball or baking a flaky pie crust.

"Certain folks in our family have special Gifts, Bone." Mamaw leveled the burdock root at her. "I can see what a plant will do to a human body." She closed her eyes again. "This one makes more fluid flow through the blood vessels and carry the bad stuff with it." She described how she saw the fluid rising in the blood and passing through the kidneys.

"Were you always able to see that?" Bone tried but didn't feel anything from the root in her hand.

"No, the Gift comes on about your age. It might come on gradual or all of a sudden. When I was twelve, Mama and me were out picking moss and ginseng up here in the woods. My fingers brushed across a leaf of deadly nightshade, and I about had a convulsion." Mamaw shook off the memory. "After that

I'd have funny feelings about certain plants when I touched them. Some would make me sick or itch—or want to pee." She held up the burdock root. "But then I started seeing more of the story. And I had to practice and teach myself what everything I was seeing meant. Even now, after all these years, I can handle an herb I've been using for twenty years, and all of a sudden see another thing it does."

Mamaw expertly peeled and shaved the root into a neat little pile. She'd dry this batch of burdock out for tea, Bone knew.

Mamaw explained that one reason she had this cabin built was so she could have the quiet to meditate on the different plants, write down all their uses in all their forms, and study books on how bodies might use them. All so she could understand what her Gift was showing her.

Bone glanced up at the bookshelf that ran above the sideboard behind her grandmother. *Gray's Anatomy.* Chemistry. Biology. Bone had always thought these were her mother's nursing school books.

"Ash done the same with animals," Mamaw said. His Gift showed him what was wrong, she explained, but that wasn't always enough to help the dog or horse. When he was young, he read every book he could get his hands on and picked the brain of every farmer and vet hereabouts. And then he learned a lot in the army handling and taking care of messenger dogs in the trenches.

Uncle Ash didn't like to talk about his time in the Great War. He'd been buried alive when a shell collapsed a tunnel he was in. And that's why Ash Reed never, ever went down in the mines again.

"Your mother had the same Gift, only with people." Mamaw hesitated, like there was something else she wanted to say, but a sadness welled up in her eyes. "That's why she wanted to be a nurse." She fell quiet.

Bone's mother had attended one year of nursing school in Charlottesville. "Why did she quit?"

"We didn't have the money after the crash." Mamaw explained that was the year the stock market crashed, and the banks started failing. "Besides, she met your daddy, and you were born the next year." Mamaw smiled. "She wouldn't have traded that for a nursing degree. And she didn't need to."

Her mother had called on sick folks and seen people here in Mamaw's office on a Sunday afternoon. Then she'd drag herself back home and collapse in bed until morning. Daddy would always make Bone scrambled eggs for supper. It was the only thing he knew how to cook.

Ruby's note vexed Bone as she plucked more burdock thistles. *The Gift killed your mother.* How? Her grandmother was watching her, waiting for her to say something. *Show her,* she could hear Will thinking. The note almost twitched in her pocket. She wanted to ask Mamaw about it more than anything. Except she was afraid of the answer. What if the Gift had killed her mother? What if it could kill her? Or Mamaw? Or Ash? Bone couldn't stand losing anybody else.

"Fetch me one of those objects from the sideboard." Mamaw waved a burdock root behind her.

On the skinny side table sat a dented pocket watch, a doll, a locket, a toy truck, and a coin. "Which one?" Bone asked. She didn't know why her grandmother would have any of these things, except maybe the coin. Maybe folks had traded them in payment for Mamaw's services.

"Any one you feel strongly about." Mamaw chipped away at the burdock root.

Bone hesitated, her hand hovering over those objects, feeling the energy they put off. This was a test, and her grandmother already knew what her Gift was. Bone let out a deep breath and reached for the wooden toy truck.

It had the warmest feeling. Bone closed her eyes as she wrapped her fingers around it. The images splashed over her like a warm bath. Uncle Junior . . . no, it was a young Papaw Reed, Hawthorne Senior, was whittling this piece of wood. He was smoking his pipe as the sun was setting; the breeze smelled like tobacco and honeysuckle. A young and very pregnant Mamaw sat beside him on the tree house porch, overlooking the valley. Papaw placed the finished toy in an empty crib. The toy radiated happiness and sadness all mixed together. The excitement and expectation of a child—and the loss of one.

Bone understood. "I didn't know." She turned to face her grandmother.

"Yes, Hawthorne made that for our first child. He was so convinced it was going to be a boy. And it was. We called him Elder, but he didn't live long enough to play with this truck."

"So that's why I only saw you and Papaw. He was very happy in the making of it. I can feel him being sad, too, but the happy was stronger. It came through first."

"I'm glad to know that, Laurel. He waited until Junior was born to make another truck. He didn't want to jinx it again."

Mamaw took the wooden truck gently from Bone's hands and placed it back on the sideboard. "Now why don't you tell me more about your Gift?"

Bone relented. She told her grandmother about the arrowhead and about Will's dinner bucket.

"Yes, I heard about that."

Of course, Uncle Junior had seen the look on her face when she touched the bucket.

"Does Junior have a Gift?" Bone had never considered the oldest Reed sibling as having something special about him, at least not like Ash or Mamaw.

"He's got a nose for coal."

"What about Aunt Mattie?"

Mamaw laughed. "If she has one, she never has let on. Or she hasn't been put in the situation where her Gift might show itself. Junior didn't think he had one at all until he went down in the mines. Sometimes it skips a generation or even a whole branch of the family tree."

Had the Gift skipped Ruby, too?

"But Ash and Willow—and you, Laurel." Her grandmother pointed a freshly peeled burdock root at her. "You all take after me. We got the stronger Gifts."

"Why did you never tell me about the Gifts before?"

"Your daddy made us promise." Mamaw tossed the root into the bowl. "He don't hold with anything he can't see or feel hisself. But you need to know." She took Bone's hand as she said this.

"Did Mama's Gift kill her?" Bone whispered.

Mamaw was silent. She looked at Bone like she'd said something in another language. "What?" she finally managed to say.

Bone swallowed hard. "Ruby . . ." Bone couldn't say it. She fumbled for the note in her pocket and handed it to her grandmother.

Mamaw smoothed out the paper carefully and read the words. Her face went a shade whiter. She stared at the words for a long moment.

"Ruby gave you this?" Mamaw shook her head sadly. "That poor child. Amarantha is filling her head up with nonsense and bile. What else did she say?"

"That the Gifts come from the devil."

"Child, you know better than that." Mamaw reached into her pocket and came out with a match. She struck it on the brick of the fireplace and lit the end of the paper. Flame curled the paper like a black ribbon, and Mamaw let the ashes fall onto the hearth.

Bone felt oddly better not to be carrying around that note.

Mamaw lifted Bone's chin with long, calloused fingers. "Your mama died of the flu. Period." She kissed Bone on the forehead. "Now help me clean up."

Mamaw filled the bowl with the burdock shavings and set it on the sink to dry. Bone chucked the burdock greens into the compost bucket by the door.

"So the Gift can't hurt me?" Bone asked as they headed out the back door.

Her grandmother wrapped her in a quick hug. By then they were standing on the porch, looking over the garden. "Now we better get back up to the house and see if those boys left us some cake."

As they walked up the path, Bone realized Mamaw hadn't exactly answered her question.

11

MAMAW, STRAIGHT AS A POPLAR SAPLING, strode up the long curving walkway to the house. Bone followed more slowly, still trying to wrap her brain around what her grandmother had told her.

"Shh." Miss Spencer pressed her finger to her lips and nodded toward Uncle Ash. They were both sitting in the rocking chairs on the veranda overlooking the valley. His boots resting on the oak railing, Uncle Ash was sound asleep.

Bone crept by them to where Will was peering through her grandfather's spyglass. He held it so she could see a hawk's nest in a tree on the next ridge.

"Wake up!" Mamaw kicked Ash's chair. "You need to eat something." She was carrying a tray of tea and cakes. Bone scrambled to help her, handing everyone a slice and a cup.

Her uncle's boots slid off the railing and onto the wooden porch with a thud. "I'm up. Damn. I did not mean to fall asleep on you, Miss Spencer." He ran his fingers through his hair and yawned.

⌒꙰⌒

Mamaw hugged her extra hard before Bone left.

On the way home, Bone sat in the back of the truck with Will and the big dogs.

Did you show her the note? Will asked. His scrap of paper fluttered away as Kiawah crawled across both their laps and laid her head on Will's leg; the Catahoula's blue marbled eyes looked up at him in utter adoration as he scratched her belly. The liver-and-white pointer, Kitty Hawk, had already stretched out at their feet.

Bone nodded. Will gave her a look that clearly said "Well?" She grabbed his notepad and pencil and printed her answer, using Kiawah's rump as her desk. *Mamaw burned up the note.*

Will's eyes widened.

Quietly, Bone told him what Mamaw had said about the Gifts and her mother. Uncle Ash and Miss Spencer were too busy laughing and talking amongst themselves to hear them, but Bone still whispered.

So did the Gift kill your mama? Will asked.

"I don't know." She patted the sleeping Catahoula on the rump. The dog snored softly in reply.

As the truck bumped down the mountain, Bone mulled over what she'd learned about the Gifts. She wanted to ask Uncle Ash about his, but not in front of Miss Spencer. Did his Gift drain him if he used it too much? Is that what happened to her mother? She'd been awfully tired whenever she came home from calling on folks or seeing them at Mamaw's. But a little sleep and Daddy's scrambled eggs always put her right. Maybe some of those folks might know something. Maybe they could tell her something about her mother's gift that Mamaw didn't know—or wouldn't tell her. And maybe she had a way of finding out.

Bone shifted out from under Kiawah's weight and slid open the window to the cab. "Uncle Ash? Can you drive Miss Spencer and me to call on folks? You know, for stories?"

Uncle Ash raised an amused eyebrow at her. "I do have calls of my own to make."

Bone looked to Miss Spencer for support.

"I'd pay for gas," she offered. Corolla was curled up asleep in Miss Spencer's lap. "I wouldn't want it to be a hardship for you," she added with a smile.

Uncle Ash chuckled. "I've been flanked. And it's not particularly a hardship." He glanced at Miss Spencer.

"Thanks." Bone slid the window closed again and settled down next to Will and the dogs.

He started to write something on his pad, but Bone stopped him.

"Mama's old patients might know something about her Gift," Bone whispered. She didn't know what exactly they might know, but it felt good to have a plan.

Will nodded as she ticked off a few names. Then he mimed a bow drawn across a fiddle.

"Mr. Childress."

Kitty Hawk raised her drowsy head briefly and then laid it back down with a thunk.

"I should of thought of him," Bone whispered. He was Will's great-uncle. The older gentleman was a great storyteller, and he and his wife had been regulars of Mama's. "Good boy," she teased Will.

He shook his head and leaned back against the truck cab, closing his eyes.

That evening Bone fell asleep to the clack of Miss Spencer's typewriter deep into the night.

12

ON THE PORCH of the Scott Brothers' store, Bone pressed the cold bottle of Nehi Miss Spencer had bought her to her lips. School had dragged on forever, and Miss Spencer was champing at the bit to call on everyone around Big Vein to get their stories. Uncle Ash had run over to Radford that afternoon, so Bone was going to introduce Miss Spencer around to folks within walking distance—ending up with Mr. Childress. Bone mapped out the route in her head as cool sugary goodness trickled down her throat.

"John Scott, what kind of establishment are you running?"

Bone froze mid-swig. The unmistakable voice echoed inside the store, and seconds later Aunt Mattie came charging out.

"I expect my orders filled correctly," she hollered over her shoulder—and then promptly steamrollered smack into Bone, knocking her on her butt and showering her in grape soda.

Bone glared up at her aunt.

Aunt Mattie merely raised an eyebrow. Miss Spencer pulled Bone to her feet.

"That's one less abomination we'll have to burn." Aunt Mattie peered down at the dress. She turned on Miss Spencer and looked her up and down. "Well, bless your heart, maybe we can add your outfit to the pyre, too, dear." She smiled her thin little smile.

Miss Spencer wore sensible slacks and a jacket.

"I'd like to see you try," she replied. "*Dear.*" She returned the smile.

Aunt Mattie stormed off. Most folks in Big Vein kowtowed to her. Bone grinned.

"This will need a good long soak." Miss Spencer fussed over the purple stain all down Bone's front. "Who was that?"

"That was my aunt."

This time Miss Spencer raised her eyebrow.

∽ こ ∾

They stopped at the boardinghouse, and Bone changed into her yellow sweater and dungarees. She and Miss Spencer called on a few folks along the main road, who were happy to share stories. The only thing Bone learned, however, was that her plan was not as simple as she'd thought. It had sounded easy-peasy in her head. But now she wasn't so sure. How, when everyone is talking about haints and bears, did you casually work in a question about your dead mother and her Gift? Plus Miss Spencer was hanging on every word and writing it down in ink in her little notebook.

Finally they got to Mr. Childress's cabin. Every afternoon, come end of first shift, he was always sitting on his porch, rain or shine, watching the men straggle home after a day in the mines. He and Miss Spencer sat in the rocking chairs sipping sweet tea while Bone settled on a milk crate between them. Mr. Childress's dogs lay about her on the porch, their feet twitching in their sleep, dreaming of chasing squirrels and raccoons through the hills.

"You ever hear the one about Ashpet, Miss Spencer?" Mr. Childress asked.

She got out her notebook.

"Once there was this woman who had two daughters. And they had them a hired girl they treated awful. They even made her sleep in the ashes by the fire."

Bone shifted on the milk crate. Ashpet was not her favorite story. The girl had to get herself rescued by a prince, but at least the woman and daughters got their comeuppance at the end.

Miss Spencer scribbled away as Mr. Childress told how the hired girl was kind to the old witch woman up on the mountain. Bone was only half listening. She still couldn't figure how to steer the conversation around to her mother. She'd have to bide her time and hope the talk went her way. Bone fidgeted on the milk crate. She was not good at biding anybody's time.

When the story was over, Mr. Childress asked Bone to fetch him his fiddle. She sprang into action.

"It's over the fireplace," he called.

Bone navigated through the rapidly darkening shack. The company put widowers and single men in the smallest company houses, the ones with one room and a tiny kitchen tacked on the backside. Uncle Junior's house was identical to this one. Just like Junior, Mr. Childress's daughters were grown and married. Bone made straight for the empty fireplace and felt above the mantel for the battered instrument.

As her fingers grazed its wood, a happy jig filled her mind. She caught flashes of a young boy dancing as Mr. Childress played. His joy flowed through the fiddle.

Bone wrapped her fingers around its neck. The tune changed. It was now the sweet, mournful strains of "Amazing Grace." The cold trickle of an image splashed over her. Mr. Childress played this fiddle as a small casket was lowered into the ground.

Bone drew her fingers back. Mr. Childress played all the funerals in Big Vein. Yet this one seemed different.

"Did you find it, Bone?" Mr. Childress called from the porch.

"Yessir." She steeled herself to wrap her fingers around the fiddle again. When she did, the images and music swelled up and then broke over her as a younger Mr. Childress sank to his knees by the body of a boy, drowned by the look of him. Bone's mama was there, too, laying a hand on the child's chest. She shook her head. He was too far gone, she said. Mr. Childress drew the bow across the strings of the fiddle in a low, mournful wail. Bone almost let go, but she dove a little deeper, looking for the joy to latch onto again. Beneath that memory was a wedding march with one of his daughters all in white. Bone picked up the fiddle and felt around for the bow.

The light flicked on and Bone found herself facing a picture of a woman and the same boy over the mantel. The bow lay in front of the framed photograph.

"Daddy misses him as much as he does her," a voice said. Mr. Childress's middle daughter, Olivia White, stood in the kitchen doorway with a mixing bowl of corn bread batter in her hands. She could've been her mother in that picture.

"How did your mama die?" Bone asked.

"Same as yours," Mrs. White said. "She had the influenza. Willow sat up with her. But she couldn't save everyone." She whipped the batter with a fork. "It's a shame she died when some others didn't."

Bone pulled her mama's yellow sweater tightly around her. She saw her mother sitting by someone's bed. That person was wracked with fever. It wasn't Mrs. Childress.

"Who didn't?" Bone asked, not sure where it would lead her.

"Oh." Mrs. White blushed. "A lot of people. It was bad that year, 1936. Not bad like 1918. But bad enough." She stopped mixing the contents of the bowl. "Some man on the train from Philadelphia or Pittsburgh, I can't remember which, was sick when he got off in Big Vein looking for work. He died, though."

"Bone?" Mr. Childress called again. "Did you get lost?"

"Keep your shirt on, Daddy. Me and Bone are talking," his daughter yelled back. "You better get out there," she told Bone. "He's itching to play, and I got to get his supper made before my husband picks me up." She ducked back into the kitchen.

Bone longed to hear more. Both of them had lost their mothers to the flu, but Mrs. White wasn't saying something. Who hadn't died?

Bone grabbed the bow and carried it and the fiddle outside.

"Are you all right, child?" Mr. Childress asked as he took the instrument from her hands. "You look like you've seen a ghost." He slid the bow across the strings, creating an eerie, ghostly sound, and then worked it into a rendition of "Coal Miner's Blues."

Questions swirled around Bone as Mr. Childress played. Who had her mother saved? Not Mr. Childress's son or wife. Could she save someone from the influenza? Bone just didn't know.

A hand lighted on her shoulder, and Bone jumped up.

It was Mrs. Price. "You better get home."

13

BONE OPENED THE SCREEN DOOR and inhaled. The whole house smelled of baked ham and biscuits, with a hint of cherry tobacco and coffee.

"You know how she is, Bay," a male voice said from the kitchen. It was Uncle Junior. Exasperated.

"It ain't right," another voice said. Uncle Ash, this time. Angry. Bone had never heard him raise his voice before. "Bone needs—"

"I'll be the judge of what Bone needs," Daddy cut him off. "I'm her father. And that's that."

Bone peeked past the kitchen door and saw them all gathered around the small Formica table piled high with ham biscuits. They were not looking at one another. Her father stood with his back to the door facing her mother's brothers. Uncle Junior stared at the ham biscuits as he slumped against the icebox, and Uncle Ash was leaning his chair back with his arms crossed, staring at nothing in particular. Corolla thumped her tail against the linoleum at his feet.

Mamaw cleared her throat as she came up behind Bone.

Her father wheeled around and saw her. "I thought I told you not to take Miss Spencer across the river." He jabbed an accusing finger in Bone's direction.

Bone stepped back, almost tripping over her grandmother's boot. "I needed to talk to Mamaw."

Mamaw put a hand on Bone's shoulder to steady her.

"So she told me." Her father crossed his arms and glared at both of them.

"I told him we talked about the Gifts, Bone," her grandmother said.

"Why did you do that?" Bone turned to search Mamaw's face for an answer.

"And I told *you* she don't need to know about that nonsense." Daddy yanked Bone away from her grandmother. He immediately let go of her. "I'm sorry, honey," he murmured.

Bone tried to fade into the wallpaper anyhow. Her father had never laid a finger on her in anger. She didn't know what to think. She was torn between wanting to escape and needing to find out what the heck was going on. Curiosity won.

Uncle Ash sprang to his feet. "Bay, you know it's not nonsense. Willow had the Gift."

Her father recoiled and then came back at Ash with his words.

"Willow *thought* she had this ridiculous gift—and look where it got her." He spat out the words he was so angry.

"Bayard Lee Phillips!" Mamaw exclaimed.

Uncle Ash looked like he'd been gut punched as he sank back into his chair.

Bone stared at her father, confused. Did he think the Gift killed her mother—even though he didn't believe in it? Bone looked to Mamaw, who shook her head ever so slightly.

Uncle Junior stepped between the other two men. "Calm down now, Bay."

"I'm sorry." Her father turned away. He braced himself on the kitchen sink while he took a deep breath. "But Bone is going to stay at Mattie's while I'm gone."

"What?" Now Bone felt like she'd been punched. This had been what they'd been arguing about all along. "No!"

"Not now, Bone." Her father faced her. "We'll talk about this later."

"I am not going to live with Aunt Mattie," Bone insisted. "Why can't I stay here? Or at Mamaw's?" It hadn't occurred to her that she'd have to leave the boardinghouse.

"We'll talk about this later." Her father's voice was sharp.

Hands maneuvered Bone out of the kitchen. "Come on, Bone, honey. Go wash up for dinner and let your daddy and the boys cool down a bit." Mamaw gave her a gentle shove toward the stairs.

Bone dragged herself up to her room.

Then Mamaw's low, determined voice scolded someone—maybe everyone—in the kitchen. Bone couldn't make out the words, but there was no mistaking the tone. Bone had a vague hope that Mamaw could make everything all right.

Bone splashed her face in the washbasin. Then she gathered up her mother's sweater and buried her face in it on the bed. The lavender scent made her feel a bit better. She pushed away a vision of Aunt Mattie speaking sharply to Bone's mother and then storming off. Bone couldn't hear the words, but they didn't matter. The ache her mama felt did. Bone felt it, too. Her father was leaving her with someone who hated her. And the stupid Gift was no help at all. Bone curled up with the sweater and cried until she was hollow inside.

A few minutes later she heard a scratching at the door. It pushed open and Corolla burst through. The fox terrier scrambled across the floor and jumped into bed beside Bone. Corolla tried to lick her face, but Bone hid under the sweater, fighting the urge to feel better in the presence of the determined dog.

"Dog, stop that." Mamaw sat down on the bed.

Corolla desisted in her efforts to uncover Bone, but she could still feel the comforting weight as the little dog pressed itself against her.

Mamaw lifted the sweater gently from Bone's face, inhaled the scent of it herself, and then laid it across Bone's shoulders. "Baby girl, your daddy has his mind made up. But, I promise you if you need me or Ash or Junior, we'll come running." Her grandmother brushed the hair out of Bone's eyes. "Sit up and let me brush your hair."

Mamaw got Bone's hairbrush off the dresser and carefully undid her ragged ponytail. Bone still fought the urge to feel better, but it was a losing battle. Her mother used to do this for her every morning.

"Your Great-grandma Daisy never cut her hair in her life." Mamaw ran a brush through Bone's hair. "I had to help her comb and plait that mess." She chuckled to herself.

"Why does he want me to live with Aunt Mattie?" Bone winced as Mamaw teased out a knot.

"He says it's because their house is closer to school and church and your friends. All of which is true." The brush pulled through Bone's hair now without a snag. Mamaw smoothed it all out until it was like corn silk.

"But you don't believe that's the real reason?" Bone asked. She didn't believe it, especially after what he'd said about her mother's Gift.

"Mattie don't hold with the Gifts. Neither does your daddy, but for entirely different reasons." Her grandmother's strong hands divided her hair into sections.

"Why does she hate the Gifts?"

Mamaw began braiding Bone's hair. Finally, she said, "Jealousy is some of it, I imagine. But there's more to it than that."

"Because she didn't get one?" Bone tried to turn but her grandmother pulled tight on the strands. "Why does she hate me?"

Mamaw wove Bone's hair back and forth several more times before answering. "She doesn't hate you. But I'll tell you a secret about grown-ups, Bone. They get scared and hurt the same as children. Only most don't throw a fit and have done with it. They hold on to the hurt and the fear—and it festers. And it comes out in peculiar ways." Mamaw caught the braid up in a rubber band. "There."

Bone did not feel comforted by this knowledge. But her stomach grumbled, and Mamaw chuckled again.

"Let's get you some supper, child."

Corolla herded Bone down the steps; Mamaw followed.

Uncle Ash was waiting for them. "How's my Forever Girl?" He wrapped her in his arms.

"Are you all staying for supper?"

Ash shook his head. "I think you and your daddy need a little time together this evening. Right, Junior?"

Mamaw nodded. "I got a stew on the stove back home." Then she hugged Bone, laid a hand on her daddy's shoulder, and showed herself out.

Uncle Junior took the hint. He gave Bone a hug, too, but not before he'd grabbed a couple ham biscuits and stuffed them in his pockets. "See you at work tomorrow, Bay," he said as he ducked out the back door.

Uncle Ash studied Bone, and she studied him right back. Everyone said the Great War changed Uncle Ash. But Bone had never known him any different, and no one ever said what had changed in him.

"Bay, we'll watch after Bone, but—" Uncle Ash tore his eyes away from Bone's. "We'll abide by your wishes. You don't need to worry about home while you're over there fighting the war."

Daddy nodded. Ash stuck out his hand, and Bone's father shook it. Then Ash kissed Bone on the forehead before he headed toward the door.

As the screen door swung shut, Bone dashed after him. "Uncle Ash?"

He looked up at her from the bottom porch step.

"Is it awful?" Bone whispered.

"Is what awful, Forever Girl?" Uncle Ash climbed back up the stairs to stand beside her.

"War," she said even quieter than before.

Uncle Ash steadied himself on the handrail before he answered. He took in a deep breath and motioned for her to sit on the top step. He hunkered down beside her. "I ain't gonna lie to you, Bone. Ever." He lit a cigarette, even though his hand was shaking. "It is. Awful. I was young and stupid when I ran off to Canada in 1914 to join up with the Expeditionary. That was three years before the U.S. got into the war." Uncle Ash stubbed his cigarette out on his boot. "My regiment saw some of the worst battles of the Great War. But this is a different war, Bone. There won't be trenches. And your father isn't stupid. He knows what he's getting into. I got a feeling he'll be okay."

He unwrapped what was left of the paper and let tobacco fall into the dirt before he stuffed the rest of his Lucky Strike back into his shirt pocket. "This is one of the first things you learn how to do in the army." Uncle Ash cracked a tiny smile in the moonlight. "How to field strip your cigarette so you don't leave a trace of where you been."

His right hand was still shaking a bit, and Bone was sorry she'd asked him about the war. The tears were coming again. She loved her uncle, but she couldn't bear the idea of her daddy being different when this war was said and done. It made her shaky inside.

Bone pushed the thought deep down and searched for a story to make them both feel better. She was ready to feel better.

"Uncle Ash." Bone sniffled back some tears. "You ever hear the story of the spirit dog and the silver mine?" She knew he had; he'd been the one to tell her.

"Aw, Forever Girl." Uncle Ash wrapped his arm around her. "You and me will get through this war just fine. Even if Mattie is more formidable than Kaiser Wilhelm," he added in a hushed voice.

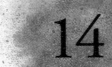

14

THE NEXT DAY, Uncle Ash drove Bone and Miss Spencer to
visit some folks across the river. All of them had been Mama's
patients. Mr. Harless at the Parrott Hardware store told them
about Frankie Silver, this notorious woman who'd murdered her
husband with an axe. Bone didn't care for those kinds of stories.
They were too often true.

Besides, she was more interested in what Mamaw sent Mrs.
Harless. Uncle Ash swapped her a small paper bag marked "Ruth
H." for some rubber tubing and other things she had set aside.
While her husband told Miss Spencer the story, Mrs. H. carried
the sack to the little woodstove in the back of the store. Bone fol-
lowed. Mrs. H. took out a pinch of dried green leaves, sprinkled

them into a chipped yellow teacup, and poured hot water over them from the kettle on the stove. A fragrant steam billowed out of the cup, but Bone didn't recognize the scent.

"What tea did Mamaw make you?" Bone asked, peering into the paper bag. Most of Mamaw's herbal concoctions looked the same to Bone.

"Stinging nettle," Mrs. Harless said with an air of relief in her voice. She breathed in the steam and took a tentative sip, which made her scrunch up her eyes a bit. "Tastes like new mown grass," she added with a wink. "But does my arthritis a world of good." She flexed her fingers, and her joints crackled.

"You used to visit Mamaw and my mother on a Sunday, didn't you?"

Mrs. Harless smiled. "Why yes, of course. Seems like yesterday to me, but it was half a lifetime ago for you." Mrs. Harless eased herself into the rocking chair by the woodstove, careful not to spill her tea. She motioned for Bone to sit on the crate next to her. "Your mama could poke and prod a person a few times and tell exactly what was wrong with them. She knew my sister's girl had an appendix that was about to burst. Had Ash drive her straight to the emergency room in Radford and got there in the nick of time. That one year of nursing school—and your grandmother—taught her more about what ails people than four years at medical school learns most doctors."

"Bone?" Uncle Ash called. "You ready to go?"

Bone started to rise, but Mrs. Harless waved her back down.

"You thinking about following in your mama's footsteps? Or maybe Mother Reed's?" She whispered, "Ash is fine with animals, but we miss your mama around here."

"Me, too," Bone admitted. She brushed the cuff of her yellow sweater against her cheek, catching the faintest whiff of lavender. And as she did, she saw gnarled hands lying in hers. Or were they her mother's hands? The arthritic fingers relaxed and opened like a flower unfurling in the sunshine.

"It's okay to miss her, honey." Mrs. Harless patted Bone on the head, and the story disappeared.

Mrs. Harless took a long sip of her nettle tea, now having the consistency of pond scum. "That other daughter of Acacia's sure as heck ain't going to carry on the family traditions. Mattie always thought she was too good for this side of the river anyhow. Your mama, though, was a fine woman. That influenza was too much for anybody to handle . . ."

"Handle?" Bone asked.

"Bone?" Her uncle had come to find her.

"Hold your horses, Ash Reed," Mrs. Harless said. "The girl wants to know about her mama."

She did want to know. More than anything. Bone was hungry to hear about anything having to do with her mother. She made puppy-dog eyes at Uncle Ash to give them another minute, but he wasn't looking at her.

It was like the older woman had slapped him. He backed toward the front of the store. "We'll wait for you outside, Bone."

Mrs. Harless shook her head. "That boy ain't been right since the last war."

"There's nothing wrong with Uncle Ash." Bone pushed herself up from the crate. "Ma'am," she added quickly before following her uncle out to the truck.

Miss Spencer was already in the passenger seat, scribbling away in her notebook. Uncle Ash paused with his hand on the door handle. "Bone, you know you can talk to me about Willow, don't you?" He wasn't looking at her.

Bone nodded. She figured she could talk to Uncle Ash about most anything and that he probably understood better than anyone what she wanted to know. Even if she wasn't sure herself what that was yet, making it all the harder to ask. Bone slid across the driver's seat next to Miss Spencer—and Corolla. But Mrs. Harless wasn't exactly wrong about Uncle Ash.

He fumbled for another cigarette and stared off into the hills for a minute before lighting it and climbing into the truck. He felt far away, like he did sometimes, even though he was sitting right there. Corolla wiggled across Bone to plant herself in her master's lap.

The yellow truck puttered back along the river road toward Goodwin's ferry in silence. Bone played with the radio knob but couldn't pick up anything good. Uncle Ash disappeared a little bit every time the subject of her mother's death came up. And that made it the hardest of all to ask him about her—and about what Ruby had said.

Miss Spencer looked up from her notes. "Ash, weren't you going to tell me about the spirit dogs?"

Bone gaped at Miss Spencer. If anything could pull her uncle back to the here and now, it was his dog stories. He loved any folktale or story about dogs, particularly black ones. Not that any of his were that color.

"There's a lot of tales about spirit or devil dogs," Uncle Ash began. He had the window rolled down, and Corolla was hanging her head out of the truck as they drove back toward Big Vein. "Sometimes the dog is a portent of death. Sometimes she's a bringer of justice. Sometimes she's both."

Uncle Ash lit another cigarette before he dove into the story. Bone unwrapped a peppermint stick her uncle had got her at the filling station in Dry Branch. Miss Spencer had offered to pay for the gas, but Uncle Ash told her he had an arrangement with the proprietor, Mr. Burman, on account of curing his dairy cows of mastitis. Uncle Ash blew a smoke ring out the window and then started talking. Miss Spencer was poised with her pen and stenographers' notebook to jot down his words in shorthand.

"A rich old man owned a passel of slaves. He was a wicked man. He had four or five wives. One would take sick and die suddenly, leaving him much richer than before. Then he'd marry him another one, and the same thing would happen."

Bone could swear her uncle stole a glance at Miss Spencer as he took a drag on his cigarette. She was writing away but looked up as soon as he turned back to the road. Bone twirled the peppermint stick in her mouth until it formed a sharp point.

"Now, he was also a cruel master," Uncle Ash continued. "He'd work his slaves to death and then leave them where they fell. He'd starve and torture them to entertain himself.

"Well, the wicked old man was finally on his death bed. His neighbors, being neighbors, set up with him, waiting for the end. At the stroke of midnight, there was scratching at the door. One of the neighbors opened it, and this big black dog bounded through. He jumped right on the bed and stared into the old man's eyes."

The scribbling stopped as Miss Spencer got caught up in Uncle Ash's story. He noticed, too, looking once more in her direction. She blushed and got real interested in writing again. Bone bit the point off the peppermint stick and crunched it between her teeth.

"'It's the devil come to take me,' the man screamed. He dropped plumb dead. The black dog trotted right back out the door and vanished."

By then, they'd reached the river crossing, and the ferry was pulling up to the dock. As they crossed the river, Uncle Ash told them another tale, this one about a dog who warned the person that death was coming. Miss Spencer forgot all about writing that one down. And Uncle Ash seemed his old easy self again.

"Uncle Ash, you ever seen a spirit dog?" Bone licked the peppermint from her fingers. It was far easier to ask him about this kind of thing.

Uncle Ash didn't say anything at first.

Miss Spencer peered at him, too, waiting for an answer.

"On two occasions," he finally said, flicking his cigarette onto the road. "Once during the war, I saw a black dog come out the mists of no-man's-land between the trenches and head toward our side. I thought we were done for."

He paused, a sly grin on his face. "But it turned out to be one of the German messenger dogs that got lost."

"What did you do with it?" Miss Spencer asked.

"Well, I fed her supper with our dogs, and then we sent her back to the Germans during a Christmas truce."

"What was the other time?" Bone asked.

The grin slid right off Uncle Ash's face, and he took even longer to answer this time. "About six years ago. Outside Mattie's house when she had the influenza. I saw this black dog walk through the front gate and disappear. Thought I was coming down with the flu myself and was seeing things." He fished out another cigarette but didn't light it. His hand even shook a bit. "But Mattie must have scared the devil dog off when it came to claim her." Uncle Ash laughed a little uneasily. "You know how she is."

Aunt Mattie could send a harbinger of death packing, even from her deathbed.

15

A BLACK SEDAN STOOD OUTSIDE the Whitakers' house
the next day.

Clay's older brothers, Carmen and Cliff, had gone down
with their ship in a place called Guadalcanal, Daddy told Bone
that evening. The Japanese torpedoed their aircraft carrier,
drowning 192 sailors. Now everyone in the boardinghouse
gathered around the radio in the parlor, waiting to hear more
news of the war in the Pacific. Somewhere off in that big ocean,
men kept on fighting—and the poor Whitaker boys lay at its
bottom.

Bone and her father pored over a map. The tiny islands in
the Pacific were so far away, and the ocean was so vast. It could
swallow up everybody she'd ever known.

The newsman on the radio was talking about the Nazis and Russians fighting near Stalingrad. Her father pointed it out on the map. Things weren't going so well in the war, Bone gathered. And her daddy would be in the thick of it in less than a week. At least, he'd be on his way.

Bone pulled the yellow sweater tight around her.

Something banged in the kitchen.

"Go help Mrs. Price," Bone's father said. "I'll call you if there's news."

In the kitchen, Mrs. Price was putting a pound of flour and a pound of sugar in a box for the Whitakers. "Pounding for the Whitakers." She dried her eyes on her apron.

Bone poured a pound of dried pinto beans into another sack and tied it off.

Everyone, every household in Big Vein, would bring the Whitakers what they could spare. A pound of this. A pound of that.

"I can't imagine losing two sons at once." Mrs. Price put the pinto beans in the box. She dried her eyes again. She and Mrs. Whitaker were good friends and cousins once or twice removed.

Clay was now the oldest Whitaker boy, and the youngest was in diapers.

"I'll take it over," Bone said. When she scooped up the box, a flash of her mother carrying another pounding box long ago hit her, but Bone pushed the image from her head. It had been for Will and his mother.

Bone met Jake's mother, Mrs. Lilly, on the way over to the Whitaker cottage. She was none too happy either.

As they came up the walk, Bone saw the boys—Clay, Jake, and Will—were sitting out on the steps talking seriously about something. Well, Will was scribbling out his answers in his notebook and showing them what he wrote—until he noticed Jake's mother. Will stuffed his notebook back in his pocket. The other boys jumped up to take the boxes.

Clay and Jake carried them in and set them on the table next to the other boxes. Bone followed, meaning to pay her respects to Clay's mother. She wasn't there. His grandmother and aunts were sorting through the pounds of dried beans, coffee, and flour while the little ones played in the parlor. And Ruby was there quietly unpacking a box of canned goods. Mrs. Lilly jumped in to help the older ladies with the sorting.

"Hey," Bone said as Ruby scooted past, box in hand, on her way out the door.

"Hey," Ruby muttered back and was gone.

That was how it was going to be, living with Ruby. It gave Bone a hollow feeling in her gut.

"Thank your mama for the canned peaches, Miss Ruby," Clay's grandmother called after her. "Just like her mother," the older woman clucked to Mrs. Lilly.

"You know what they say about apples," Mrs. Lilly agreed.

Bone and the boys snuck back outside and joined Will on the steps.

As soon as the door shut, Will brought out his notebook again and finished writing something.

"That much?" Clay asked.

Bone peered at Will's paper. It said *$1.20 a car*. Then he scribbled, *when you get a full share.*

"Hey, you're not—," Bone said.

Jake rounded on Bone. "You got to swear to keep this a secret."

"But you can't." She looked at Clay.

"They let Will, and my daddy started in the mines at my age," Clay cut her off, daring Bone to say anything more.

Bone wanted to say that Clay wasn't Will's age, but she didn't. Will was two years older than Clay.

Will wrote some more. Bone saw . . . *sorting pays less.*

"But why do you want to go down the mines?"

"I can't join up yet, so I got to do something." Clay fought back the tears, and Jake put an arm around him.

Bone felt like crying, too. They sat there in silence for a moment.

Clay blew his nose in his sleeve. "I heard Mama and Daddy saying last night how we're only getting by," Clay whispered. "And now we won't have Carmen's and Cliff's pay they sent home. I got to do something."

"It ain't fair."

Will wrote down something. *I'll look after them.*

Them? She looked at Jake. Of course, wherever Clay Whitaker went so did Jake Lilly.

"Don't tell anyone," Jake begged.

Bone jumped to her feet. Jake and Clay and Will all in the mines. One little accident could take them—and her father and Uncle Junior for that matter—out with one fell swoop.

The hollow feeling ate at her gut.

"I got homework," she said, her lip quivering. She scrambled down the steps, pulled her sweater tight around her, and headed back to the boardinghouse. She pushed away an image of her mother watching Uncle Ash go off to war. Bone wanted to tear the sweater off and never put it back on. And then again, she didn't. It was like Mama was here, nudging her along. Only Bone didn't always want to hear what she had to say.

A few minutes later, the crunch of size 10 boots came up behind her on the gravel road. Will pressed a note into her hands.

Were you this upset when I went down the mines?

"I was, you fool." Bone crumpled up the note and tossed it back at him. "But you were so happy about it that I didn't want to ruin it for you. And this is different." Now she had no one. She'd be all alone in school and at home. Bone pushed Will away as he tried to put his arm around her.

The two of them walked back up to the boardinghouse without saying a word. For once, Will's rocklike silence didn't make Bone feel any better. She was sitting out in the river with only this one rock to cling to, and the water was rising fast.

16

SCHOOL WAS QUIET without Clay and Jake. The mine hired them to sort coal. It was an outside job working under Jake's father.

After another whirlwind afternoon of story collecting, Bone found herself sitting on the porch of the Scott Brothers' store with her Uncle Ash. It was the Friday before her daddy was supposed to leave for war, and Bone felt only a tad closer to figuring out what had happened to her mother.

Miss Spencer had gone inside to mail a letter. She had a thick notebook chockful of stories now. Bone hadn't made as much progress in her own private story collecting. Most people said what Mrs. Harless had. People missed Bone's mother and her uncanny ability to suss out any illness. Today, Mr. DeHart told the story of Mama diagnosing his father's bad heart. The doctors said there wasn't much that could be done. They couldn't up and give him a new heart, and none of Mamaw's herbs would fix what ailed him. So Willow sat up with him until it was near the end. Mr. DeHart didn't blame her for not being there for the dying part. That was for family.

Uncle Ash had overheard the story. "Willow didn't like to lose," he added. Mr. DeHart nodded like he understood completely.

That's what Bone was pondering as she and Uncle Ash rocked in the big white chairs on the concrete porch of the company store. She buttoned up her sweater in the cool breeze. As she did, she saw her mother pitching a fit as Uncle Ash pulled her away from a patient.

"Uncle Ash?"

"Hmm?" he answered, sounding like he was about to doze off.

"What did you mean by Mama not liking to lose? Who was she losing to?"

Uncle Ash took a long drag on his cigarette before he straightened up. "You know what your mama's favorite story was?"

Bone shrugged. Her mother had told her many, many stories when she was little.

"Soldier Jack. At least the part right before the end. You know, where Jack catches Death in the bag."

"Yes!" Bone answered. It was one of her favorite stories, too. "The king's daughter has gotten sick, and she's on her deathbed.

So Jack grabs the jar and the magic sack the old man had given him—"

"Did I miss a story?" Miss Spencer asked as she handed Bone a cold grape Nehi. She settled into the rocking chair next to Uncle Ash with an RC Cola of her own.

"I'll tell you the rest later, India," Uncle Ash whispered to her. He turned back to Bone. "Go on, Jack spies Death through the jar—"

"Old Death is standing at the foot of her bed, and Jack orders him into the sack," Bone took up the story with relish. "The king's daughter wakes up. He hangs that sack from a high tree, and then him and the daughter get married and lived happily ever after."

"That's where Willow always liked to leave off." Uncle Ash reached into his pocket for something.

"There's more?" Bone asked. She didn't remember anything else coming after the happily ever afters.

"Yes." Ash grinned. "Jack and the king's daughter do get married and do live for quite a long time. In fact, everybody does. Death's trapped up in the tree. Nobody dies. Babies keep getting born, but people keep getting older and older. And the world keeps getting more and more crowded. Soon Jack's wife comes to him and says he's got to let Death out of the sack. She's awful tired. They can't go on like this. Jack is eventually convinced. He lets Death down from the tree and opens up the sack. He and his wife pass away right on the spot."

Miss Spencer rifled through her notes.

Bone raised the Nehi to her lips to take a sip and think on the story a bit, but the bottle cap was still on. "Are you saying that Mama didn't like to lose to Death?" Bone finally asked.

Uncle Ash nodded as he reached for her bottle. "And she always said, 'It cost too much to keep Death in the bag.' I never quite knew what she meant by that." Uncle Ash flipped open the army knife he'd fished out of his pocket. "It's hard on me when an animal dies, but sometimes, a lot of the time, it's kinder to let them go. Mostly there's nothing I can do about death. It'll come when it comes."

His hand shook a bit when he popped off the bottle cap with the opener and handed the grape soda back to Bone. She took a thirsty gulp of it while she considered her mother's peculiar words. Could Mama do something about death? She shook her head. That was silly. Wasn't it?

"When are you going back to Roanoke?" Uncle Ash asked Miss Spencer as he opened her RC Cola. Then he lit a fresh cigarette, and Corolla settled at his feet.

"Before Thanksgiving. I'm teaching three sections of American History come January, and I'd like some time to go through all these stories before then." Miss Spencer flipped through her notebook. "I never dreamed we'd get so many different ones. I don't want them to end up moldering away in some office in Richmond."

Bone reckoned they'd hit up everyone on both sides of the river. And they'd gotten a smattering of every kind of story: Jack tales, Cherokee legends, frontier stories, true crime, Gypsies, and the lot. But as she spied Oscar Fears and Tiny Sherman making their way up the road to the mine, Bone smacked her forehead. She'd forgotten about the folks of Sherman's Forest. "Miss Spencer, you're missing a whole bunch of good stories." *And some of my mother's best customers.* Bone waved. "Hey, Mr. Fears, Mr. Sherman."

"Hey, Miss Bone." They headed her way.

"Bone, don't—" Miss Spencer shifted uneasily in her chair.

It was too late. Bone had already leapt up and met the two men halfway.

"Miss Spencer here is collecting folktales and such for the WPA. Y'all got time to tell her one of the Br'er Rabbit stories?"

Mr. Sherman's face lit up.

Mr. Fears laughed. "Tiny always got time for a story." He headed on to the change house.

"I'd love to, Miss Bone, but maybe some other time," Mr. Sherman answered. He already had on his bank clothes, but instead of a miner's cap, he wore a red baseball cap that said *Memphis.*

Uncle Ash rose and shook Mr. Sherman's hand. "Always good to see you, Tiny. Ya'll want a pop or a smoke?"

Mr. Sherman took one look at Miss Spencer and removed his cap. "Thanks, Ash, but I ain't got too long before I need to be at the mantrip."

The evening shift started in about fifteen minutes. Daddy, Uncle Junior, and Will would be heading down this way soon.

"You work at the mine?" Miss Spencer blushed. "I'm sorry. I didn't mean—"

"Ma'am, I know exactly what you meant," Mr. Sherman said carefully but not unkindly. "But we got this saying down in the mine. We all the same color under all that coal."

Ash laughed, and so did Miss Spencer, if a bit more slowly.

"Y'all coming to the game Sunday?" Mr. Sherman asked. "I'm pitching, and Miss Bone—" Mr. Sherman lightly swatted Bone's shoulder with his Memphis Red Sox cap. "Will is playing left field, and them other friends of yours are warming the bench."

As the ball cap touched her, Bone could see Tiny standing on the pitcher's mound. The sun beat down. Sweat trickled into his eyes. He reared back and threw a fastball. The crowd roared. A grin flickered across his face as he wiped his brow. Then he tugged his cap back down tight and threw another strike.

The Memphis Red Sox cap fluttered toward the ground, and Bone, without thinking, caught it. Images rushed over her like rainwater after a heavy storm, cold and raw as early spring. White faces were calling Tiny names she could never repeat. He was lying on the ground, held down by two of the white boys. The others smashed their boots into Tiny's right arm over and over. She felt pinned down by the backwash of memories, unable to look away from the terrible sight of him bloodied and beaten. She was powerless to help him or herself. Then the image faded away, and she smelled the familiar scent of lavender.

"Thank you, Miss Bone." Mr. Sherman took the ball cap gently from her hand.

Bone stood blinking in the sun as the present came back into focus.

Mr. Sherman put his cap back on. "Now, if you don't mind, I got to hightail it." He jerked his thumb toward the Big Vein change house. "Miss Bone. Ma'am. Ash." He tipped the brim of his cap.

Uncle Ash nodded, but he was watching Bone.

Mr. Sherman fell in beside Tom Albert as they walked up the hill. They talked loudly about baseball. Both of them played for Big Vein. The freshly scrubbed members of the day shift began to trickle out.

"You all right, Bone?" Uncle Ash asked.

She didn't answer. The image of Mr. Sherman broken on the ground, cradling his arm, was still in her head. She tried to shrug it off, but it tugged at her. Bone needed to know more about that memory, even if she didn't want to. She was tired and sad all of a sudden.

Uncle Ash handed her a peppermint stick. "Sometimes these help. They're better for you than a Lucky Strike." He winked.

Bone bit down on the candy, and energy began to flow back into her.

Uncle Ash lit another Lucky Strike, but his eyes were still on Bone.

Miss Spencer was busy making notes in her little book.

"Uncle Ash?" Bone fought back a yawn. "Did Tiny ever get beat up real bad?"

Miss Spencer looked up.

Uncle Ash let out a long plume of smoke. "Back when he was about sixteen or seventeen, some fellows from Great Valley beat Tiny something awful. It was right after he'd gotten signed to that team in Memphis."

"The Memphis Red Sox," Bone added. It was a famous Negro Leagues team.

Uncle Ash nodded. "Those white boys broke his pitching arm. His baseball career was almost over before it began."

This was what Bone saw when she'd touched the cap. She couldn't help shivering.

Miss Spencer shook her head. "The doctor must have done a good job fixing it. He got to play, right?"

"Back then, none of the white doctors would see black folk, and the nearest colored hospital was two hours away." Uncle Ash looked at Bone. "It was a good thing your mama was home from nursing school. She was the one who fixed up Tiny's arm. She set and splinted it like a doctor herself." Uncle Ash turned away and took a long drag on his cigarette. "So, yes, Tiny got to play for Memphis after all, thanks to Willow."

But there was more to that story. Bone could feel it in the cap. Maybe Tiny's aunt who raised him could fill in the blanks.

"You know, Tiny's Aunt Queenie knows a lot of stories you ain't heard yet," Bone said to Miss Spencer.

"I could run you all over to Sherman's Forest one afternoon," Ash offered as he sat down in Bone's chair. "I need to check on

Miss Queenie's mare anyways." Sherman's Forest was where the black people lived.

Miss Spencer tidied up her notes and stuffed them into her bag before she answered. "Um, the WPA told me not to collect stories in nonwhite communities. A couple of black writers are doing that in the Tidewater area."

Uncle Ash nodded. "Might be best."

"But Aunt Queenie won't mind," Bone said. "She's told me all sorts of stories." She needed to talk to Aunt Queenie about Mama. Bone knew it. Uncle Ash used to drive her and her mother (and Mamaw) over to Sherman's Forest all the time to see people and animals.

"We don't want to get Miss Spencer in trouble with her boss now, do we?" Uncle Ash said to Bone.

"No," Bone relented. "Could I go with you to see Aunt Queenie's mare?"

"What are you up to, Bone?" Uncle Ash crossed his arms.

Bone about choked on the last of the peppermint stick. He handed her the Nehi, which she gulped down as she thought of a reply. The combination of grape soda and mint burned going down. She grimaced, and Uncle Ash tried not to smile. Bone wanted to tell him everything. But she couldn't. Not yet. Uncle Ash might not be able to bear it. "Nothing."

"Uh-huh," Uncle Ash remarked, but he let it drop. He turned to Miss Spencer. "Do you like baseball? Big Vein is playing Great Valley at Centennial Park Sunday afternoon."

Centennial Ballpark was this ball field the mines had built between Big Vein and Great Valley. All mines had a team. If Mr. Sherman was playing, all of Sherman's Forest—including Aunt Queenie—would be at the game. Bone could sneak over and talk to her then. A yawn escaped Bone.

Uncle Ash raised an amused eyebrow at her. Maybe he already knew what she was up to. Maybe he knew how tired she felt at the moment. "Shall I pick y'all up after church?" he asked Miss Spencer.

She smiled at Uncle Ash.

The image of a young black man, not much older than Will, getting beaten by white men still lingered in Bone's brain. She felt a teeny tiny bit closer to unraveling her mother's secrets. There was more to that story. Bone felt it in the ball cap.

But first she needed a nap.

17

DADDY LAID TWO SILVER HALF-DOLLARS on the kitchen table in front of Bone. She stopped shoveling oatmeal into her mouth. "Why ain't . . . aren't you at work?" It was Saturday, the last Saturday before he was supposed to leave, but it was still a workday. Daddy never missed work.

"What are they going to do? Fire me?" Daddy looked especially pleased with himself. "I'm playing hooky to take my best girl to the pictures." He pushed one of the half-dollars toward Bone. On it, Lady Liberty was walking toward the sun.

Bone picked up the coin. She could feel the warmth of Daddy's hand still on it—and she could see him carefully wiping off the coal dust and setting coins aside every payday just for her. The silver was made of coal, sweat, and love.

Bone slapped the coin down on the table and pushed it back toward Daddy. She was still mad at him. He was still leaving her, and with Aunt Mattie, of all people. He still hadn't talked to Bone about it.

Daddy tapped the coin. "This should cover a matinee, some popcorn, and maybe even a chocolate soda at the drugstore."

"In town?" Bone gulped down the oatmeal. "You mean a movie at the Lyric?" She'd never been to a real movie theater before. The mine showed movies during the summer on the croquet field and sometimes in the church hall during the winter. The pictures were at least six months behind what the folks in town saw.

"I borrowed Henry's car. Go put on one of your school dresses." Bone raced up the stairs.

"What are we going to see?" Bone asked, climbing into the front seat of the big black Ford. She tugged on her yellow sweater over her blue and green plaid feed sack dress.

"You look nice, Laurel," Daddy said before he threw the car into gear. "The main feature is some cartoon about a deer."

"A deer?" Bone asked, trying to keep the disappointment out of her voice. She'd been hoping for a Sherlock Holmes or another Katharine Hepburn movie.

"That's what's playing." Daddy shrugged.

The car bumped down the gravel mine road, past the river, and onto the main road to town. Daddy seemed a million miles away as they wound through the hollows. Bone wanted to confront him about staying with Mattie. He'd said they'd talk about it. They hadn't. At first Bone avoided him, and then he was busy with work or talking to Uncle Junior about work. And now . . . And now she didn't want to spoil her first movie in a real movie theater.

"How 'bout some music?" Daddy asked.

Bone turned the dial until she found something. The twinkly sound of a piano answered by jazzy brass poured out of the radio. It was the kind of music you heard in movies.

"That's Glenn Miller! 'Pardon me, boys,'" Daddy crooned along with the music. Bone giggled. His voice was deep and scratchy, good, but like he hadn't used it in years. By the time they pulled into town and parked across from the theater, Daddy had serenaded Bone to Glenn Miller, Harry James, Tommy Dorsey, and several jingles. It was like being part of her own Hollywood musical.

And the movie theater was grand. A marquee with bright letters jutted out over the sidewalk. Big glass doors swung into the lobby. The floor was real red carpet, and a boy in a smart uniform took tickets and popped popcorn. Bone and her daddy settled down in cushioned seats just as the maroon velvet curtains parted. The black-and-white newsreel lit up the screen.

Both Daddy and Bone leaned forward to watch as the troops headed toward Alaska. They marched through the snow, but in the end, they still had mail call, church, and even dances up there. It seemed more like camp than war. Bone sighed a bit, and Daddy put his arm around her.

They laughed through the Looney Tunes. Then Superman spotted Nazis with his X-ray vision, and their bullets bounced off the Man of Steel.

The curtains pulled wider, and the main feature started. Bone stuffed popcorn into her mouth as Bambi took his first wobbly steps. The mother deer was beautiful. The little deer frolicked with his friends. They spotted the Great Prince deer in the woods.

"I bet that's his father," Bone whispered.

Both she and her daddy tensed as the Man entered the forest with his gun.

Bone felt the crack go through her as the Man shot Bambi's mama. Hot tears welled up inside her, and the popcorn slid to the floor. "Daddy, can we go?" she heard herself whisper. Bone shivered in the dark, the memory of the real deer drowning in the river washing over her. Daddy whisked Bone out to the lobby. He dried her tears with his hankie. It smelled of cherry tobacco and Ivory Soap. "I'm sorry, Bone honey. I had no idea what the movie was about. We can go back in if you want. Or we can get an ice cream soda."

As much as Bone loved the movie theater, a chocolate soda beat out a story about a dead mama deer any day. The cool air outside the theater made her feel a bit better as they walked the block to Central Drug.

⁓

Bone spun around once on the candy apple red stool and took in the drugstore lunch counter. Daddy pored over the newspaper he'd bought on the way in. The guy in the paper hat mixed Bone's chocolate soda. The black-and-white floor gleamed. Young men in crisp uniforms perched on other stools. They laughed and flirted with the girls with them. The boys looked like the soldiers in the newsreel, going off to war like it was church camp.

"Daddy, are those soldiers shipping out with you?" Bone asked, nodding to the young fellows.

Daddy looked up from the paper. "No, they're cadets at the college. They won't be real soldiers until they graduate."

One of the cadets glared at Daddy.

"I expect the war will be over by then," Daddy added. "There are worse places to spend the war than in school."

Like Aunt Mattie's house. "Daddy, why do I have to stay with her?"

He sighed and folded up the paper. The guy in the paper hat set a cup of coffee in front of Daddy and a tall chocolate soda topped with whipped cream in front of Bone. "I did say we'd talk later."

"It's later." Bone stuck a straw down through the thick chocolate ice cream.

"I told you all my reasons." He ticked them off his fingers. "Henry and Mattie can give you a good home. Ruby will be there for company. Their house is close to school and church . . ."

Bone took a long, deep slurp of the chocolate soda. It was about the best thing she'd ever tasted. She almost forgot what Daddy was saying. Almost. She sucked in the icy chocolaty goodness until her head started to hurt.

He paused to watch her. "Good, huh?"

Bone nodded, pulling her sweater tight around her for warmth. She caught a flash of a memory. Mama and Daddy, both much younger, were sitting here at the drugstore arguing. *"You don't have that kind of Gift,"* he told her. Mama just smiled and shook her head at him. Bone shook herself.

"And Mattie and Henry can afford to treat you girls to a movie and soda every once in a while." Daddy was counting on his fingers again.

"You don't think the Gifts are real, do you?" Bone asked.

Daddy set his coffee cup down with a clatter and looked around to see if anyone noticed. "No, not in the way—"

"Then why does it matter where I stay?" Bone spun away from him.

Daddy took a moment to answer. Finally, he said, "Believing in something that's not real can be dangerous. Kindly like thinking you could stop bullets when you can't." He pulled Bone around to look her in the eye. "You can put yourself in a dangerous situation."

Bone sucked the bottom of the soda dry as she considered this. He had a way of making things sound so reasonable. Did he think Mama fooled herself into thinking she had a Gift? Bone stroked her sweater, but it was no help. Still, Bone was sure of what she'd experienced when she touched certain objects. Her Gift wasn't like stopping bullets or X-ray vision, but it was real. And something still didn't make sense. Aunt Mattie must believe in the Gifts.

"Aunt Mattie thinks the Gifts are the devil's work," Bone ventured.

Daddy chuckled. "I know. Some beliefs are more harmless than others. Mattie's harmless. She's more bark than bite." He drained the last of his coffee and stood up. "Ready to go home?"

Bone was not sure Daddy was entirely right about Aunt Mattie, or anything else at the moment. They rode home in silence. Not even Glenn Miller had anything more to say.

18

AS SOON AS THE LAST HYMN was sung, Bone—and about every other person in the congregation—ran home to change clothes for the last game of the season. Her daddy didn't hold with church but still made her go with Mrs. Price every week. Bone tore off her Sunday best, which Mrs. Price had made from one of her mother's old dresses, and put on her dungarees, a white T-shirt, and her yellow sweater.

Uncle Ash pulled up in his old yellow pickup as the mine truck with the players was driving past. It was an open-back monstrosity the outside men used to cart timbers down to the mill. The truck bounced down the gravel road with Junior at the wheel, the players hanging on for dear life. Will and the boys waved, and Mamaw leaned over and honked the horn back at them. She wouldn't have missed a game. Uncle Junior was team captain, like his father had been back in his day.

Uncle Ash, Mamaw, and Corolla got out of the cab of his truck.

"Is your daddy coming?" Uncle Ash asked Bone as he held the door open for Miss Spencer. She slid into her usual spot, and Corolla jumped up into her lap.

"He went with Aunt Mattie," Bone answered as she climbed into the back. She hadn't said more than five words to Daddy since they got home from the movies. Mamaw handed her a picnic basket and some blankets before she followed. Uncle Ash held out his hand to help her, but she waved it off. "And Ruby. They went early so they could set up the scrap drive," Bone added.

"Amarantha does like doing her part," Mamaw said. "And she makes sure Ruby does too, whether she likes it or not." She spread out one of the blankets for her and Bone to sit on and then handed her a still-warm slice of coffee cake from the basket as they settled in for the ride.

"Hold on, Mama." Ash backed the truck up in the yard and gunned it out into the gravel.

As they rambled down the mine road, Bone could hear the quiet strains of the country music on the radio coming from the cab. The ride smoothed out when the truck turned onto the paved river road and headed north.

"I hear you been asking about Willow," Mamaw said, out of nowhere.

"What's wrong with that?" Bone snapped.

"Not a thing," Mamaw reassured her. "I like hearing about her, too. I miss Willow as much as I do Hawthorne. Maybe more even." Mamaw brushed the crumbs from her dungarees before she continued. "Your Uncle Ash is worried about you, is all."

She reached into the picnic basket to pull out something wrapped in brown paper. There were more little brown bags and packages with folks' names scribbled on them than there was actual food in the basket. Her grandmother unwrapped the paper, revealing an old-timey-looking baseball cap. It was white with a black bill and letters that said *Big Vein*. "You know your grandfather loved baseball. He only wore this while he was playing and then he'd carefully wrap it up in butcher paper and keep it in one of my old hatboxes." She placed the cap on Bone's head before she could object. Bone squinched her eyes closed, readying herself for the cold onrush she'd felt with Tiny Sherman's cap. This time, though, the images lapped gently against her like she was floating on the river on a hot, sunny day.

Papaw's happiness washed over her as he ran, the flannel cap pulled tight down over his forehead, onto the green field. He pounded the well-oiled mitt with his fist. His heart raced when the batter stepped up to the plate. The smell of cut grass and hot dogs filled his nostrils. Salty sweat rolled down his face. He scooped up a ground ball and threw it to first.

Bone described what she saw as they pulled into the paved parking lot of Centennial Ballpark. Mamaw removed the cap from Bone's head, rewrapped it in the butcher paper, and gently placed it back in the basket. "Anytime you want, you can borrow Papaw's cap. Baseball was his church, and he was happiest when he was playing."

Mamaw was offering her a safe object to practice her Gift on, one with nothing but good memories in it.

The happy feeling lingered as Bone surveyed the ballpark. The mines hadn't slapped a diamond on a field and called it baseball. They'd built bleachers behind home plate, a concession stand, covered dugouts for the teams, and a proper scoreboard out past the cyclone fence that ringed the field.

The stands were filling up since it was a doubleheader. Some white folks were camped out on the right field side of the grass; the black folks always got the left side, and it was packed today on account of Tiny. Many of them on the left field side hadn't changed after church, so it looked like an Easter picnic was going on. Bone spotted Aunt Queenie holding court by the left field fence.

Bone carried the blankets as Mamaw made for her usual seat on the left side of the bleachers. Uncle Ash and Miss Spencer headed toward the concessions. Daddy was talking to some folks by the cold-drinks stand.

Big Vein took to the field first. Jake and Clay were the only ones left on the bench. Bone was torn between wanting to watch or sneaking over to talk to Aunt Queenie. When Uncle Ash and Miss Spencer returned with hot dogs and RC Colas, Bone figured she'd eat first. She dug into her plain hot dog. Uncle Ash didn't need to ask how she or Mamaw liked theirs. Purists, he called them. Miss Spencer favored mustard.

"Bone," Uncle Ash said. Miss Spencer interrupted him to dab a spot of chili from the corner of his mouth. He blushed a bit. "Your daddy said for you to help Mattie out with the scrap drive after a while to give Ruby a break."

"But—," Bone protested.

"Bone," Ash said patiently. "Ruby might like a chance to visit with her mamaw, too." He winked at his mother. She mouthed her thanks in return.

Bone couldn't deny her grandmother the chance to talk to Ruby without Aunt Mattie interfering.

"Okay," Bone relented. "After I see Will play a bit." She was forming a new plan.

"Fair enough." Mamaw bit contentedly into her red hot.

Bone wolfed down her own hot dog. "I'm gonna watch from the fence." She slipped out of the bleachers before Mamaw or Uncle Ash could say boo.

The crowd in the left field whooped and cheered as Tiny Sherman struck out his third batter in a row. Bone reached the chain link fence behind the dugout right as Will and the boys came running in to bat.

Uncle Junior handed Will a bat. "You're up first."

Will approached the plate, thwacked it with his bat, and relaxed into as good a batting stance as Bone had ever seen. The fastball tore down the middle of his strike zone, but Will met it with a crack. The ball peeled out of there toward the left field fence. Will took off toward first.

"He's a regular Joe DiMaggio," Uncle Junior declared.

"Run, Will," Bone yelled when he headed toward second. The Great Valley man in left field finally got to the ball and let it hurl. Will slid for it.

"Safe!" the ump declared.

Bone backed her way along the dugout fence toward the left field side, hoping people would think she just wanted a better view of Will on second. Marvin Linkous popped up to center, and his brother Garvin struck out. Then Tom Albert hit a line drive but got tagged out before he reached first.

Bone stayed by the fence, watching the game, while Aunt Queenie talked to her church deacon. Tiny was up to pitch again. He shook his head at Tom Albert's first signal but nodded at the next one. Then he reared back and unfurled that right arm as he wheeled around and snapped the ball toward home plate. The ball was like a bullet. The next thing Bone heard was the smack of it against Tom Albert's mitt. He shook out his hand before he threw the ball back to Tiny.

"Strike one," yelled the ump.

Tiny did that two more times, each seeming faster than the first.

A thought struck Bone as fast as that pitch. She'd seen his arm stomped by those white boys. How had it healed so perfect? Especially if Mama was the only one who tended to it. The bone had shattered into pieces like a broken jar.

"His pitching is as good as ever, ain't it?" Aunt Queenie stood beside Bone.

"Yes, ma'am," Bone replied. "I never seen anything so fast. Didn't he break that arm when he was about Will's age?"

"Ain't that your mama's sweater?"

Bone nodded.

"We used to see that sweater come round Sherman's Forest all the time, especially after she set Tiny's arm." Queenie placed her finger alongside her nose like she was a spy in the movies telling her a secret. "It was a regular miracle he was still able to play ball after that," she added in a whisper. "Tiny played four seasons for Memphis."

Bone touched the cuff of her yellow sweater. Her mother laid a hand on Tiny's arm for a long moment before proceeding to set it. The pain in his face eased under Willow Reed Phillips's touch.

"How you doing, Queenie?" Mamaw came up behind them with her picnic basket in tow. "You best go help Mattie now." She nodded her head toward the concession stand.

The vision disappeared, the spell broken.

Bone sighed heavily. Both women laughed like the old friends they were. They asked after each other's families and then got down to business.

"I got that burdock and ginseng you wanted," Mamaw said.

"And I got peach preserves and some of that brandy you like," Aunt Queenie countered.

"Go," both Mamaw and Aunt Queenie told Bone when they noticed she hadn't moved a muscle.

Bone dragged herself toward the scrap drive. Her head was a million miles away (and about thirteen years in the past). And the sweater was nudging her along. It was like her mother was helping her understand what had happened, one little peek at a time.

A hand snatched Bone by the ear.

"Laurel Grace Phillips," her Aunt Mattie roared at her. "What were you doing on *that* side of the grass?"

"I was talking to Aunt Queenie." The fingers gripping her ear twisted hard. "Ow."

"She is not your aunt. I am, and when you're living under my roof, you'll stay away from the wrong sort of people."

"I ain't living there yet." Bone twisted away from her aunt's grasp. "I got one more day."

"Less than that," Mattie Albert said with some satisfaction.

And she was right. Bone had a few hours left until her daddy left for Fort Benning in the wee hours of the morning. And she hadn't solved anything. She had her suspicions, but she wasn't any closer to finding out whether the Gift killed her mother. And none of it would make her daddy stay.

The water was rising around her. Soon she'd have nothing left to cling to.

Bone backed away from her aunt and took off running toward Big Vein.

19

BONE RAN UNTIL SHE COULDN'T HEAR Aunt Mattie's voice calling after her. It was only a mile or two back to the coal camp, and she'd walked to the games plenty of times before. Maybe she'd think of something as the gravel road crunched out a rhythm under her feet.

But it wasn't long before a familiar yellow pickup pulled alongside her. Uncle Ash leaned over and opened the passenger door for her.

He was alone, except for Corolla, who barked at her to get in already. Bone did and slammed the door after her.

"Try not to break my truck," Uncle Ash joked.

Bone didn't say a word.

Uncle Ash threw the truck into gear. Bone feared he'd whip around and take her back to the game to face Aunt Mattie. He didn't turn, at least until they got to the river. Then he cut the engine off. He couldn't be waiting for the ferry because it didn't run on Sunday. He'd have to drive up the river to cross at the Spruce Run bridge to get home.

"What are you hoping to accomplish with all your questions?" He fumbled for a Lucky Strike as he turned to her.

"What do you mean?" Bone was genuinely surprised. She'd expected him to reassure her, like everyone else, that everything would be all right or at least that Mattie didn't hate her. Corolla laid her head in Bone's lap and looked up at her expectantly, too.

"Mama said you were asking Queenie about Willow." Uncle Ash tapped an unlit cigarette against the dash. "And it hasn't escaped my notice that you've been using our story-collecting jaunts for your own devices. Not that I mind, but I'm curious."

Bone shrugged. The water of the New River rushed past them with no way to cross it. She wanted to tell him but still wasn't sure she should or could. She was out of time, as Mattie so unkindly reminded her.

"What is it that you're trying to figure out?" Uncle Ash stuck the cigarette in his mouth but didn't light it.

"Did the Gift kill my mother?" Bone blurted out.

Uncle Ash chucked the unlit smoke out the window. "You shouldn't be scared of your own Gift, Bone."

"That's—" She was going to say that wasn't it at all. But it was true. She was scared.

Uncle Ash shushed her gently. "The only thing that'll hurt you is *not* learning how to use it. I've been remiss in my duties as an uncle, Forever Girl. I've been remiss in a lot of things. But whatever you need to know about your mama, maybe you're looking in the wrong places. Maybe you oughta look to your own Gift. Her Gift was a big part of your mother's life."

He took out another Lucky Strike and lit it this time. Bone opened her mouth but didn't quite know what to say. He went on without noticing. His eyes were on the river now.

"It runs through us like that river out there. Willow had an ease in her Gift. When I came back from the war, she showed me that I could use mine—like she did hers—to do real good. That kept me going. It still does."

Bone felt like that muddy river was fixing to carry her away.

He started the truck's engine again. "I'll still come get you and India after school to collect stories, and you can come visit your mamaw anytime you want. Tell you what. I'll meet you at the store after school every day."

"Take me home with you now?" Bone had been hoping that Uncle Ash might steal her away to Reed Mountain to live in the tree house, like the Little People stole away the Forever Boy.

"Aw, Forever Girl, I can't do that," he said. "I promised your daddy we'd abide by his wishes after he leaves. Besides, you gotta give the Big People a chance first."

"But Aunt Mattie hates me," Bone let out. Corolla nudged Bone.

"She don't hate you." Uncle Ash turned to Bone. "Now she doesn't like me much." He chuckled. "But she loved Willow, despite what most people think. She loved her more than most anybody, except maybe Ruby. And Willow loved her.

"You ask that sweater of yours," he whispered. "It saw everything."

Bone couldn't take it anymore. She wanted things to stay like they were—before the Gift, before that stupid note of Ruby's, before that darned draft notice. The river inside of her was carrying her somewhere she didn't want to go.

Bone got out of the truck and ran up the mine road and into Flat Woods. As she raced through the woods, the now orange and red leaves fell around her like early snow. Sun streamed in from above. The woods were quiet except for the distant chugging of a train.

Bone ran on. She ran past Picnic Rock and along the flats. She ran until she stumbled into a foxhole, the same one she'd hid in before.

She stretched out in the hole, her own ragged breath the only sound in the forest. Above her the trees were a bit barer, and the leaves glowed in the setting sun. Eighty years ago, men lay in this same spot to avoid being swept off to a war they didn't want to fight. How many had avoided the press-gangs? How many got to stay home and tend their crops and be with their families—like before the war? Maybe if she hid out here Aunt Mattie couldn't find her. Maybe her daddy couldn't leave. Deep down, though, she couldn't do that to him.

She dug around in the dirt with her hand, searching for that coin she'd touched before. She found it and braced herself for the images. They didn't come right away. She held it up, brushing away the dirt with her fingers. It was an old nickel. Well, it looked like a nickel, but it had III on the back.

Bone wrapped her hand around the three-cent piece and closed her eyes. The scene flowed around her and she let herself be pulled along with it. A man clutched this silver coin. It had been summer. The leaves blocked out the sky above, and the air sweltered. The hole was cool against his back. He tossed the coin in the air to entertain himself. A voice whispered, "They're coming," and he snatched the coin from the air and burrowed deeper under the cover of his hole.

Horses and men picked their way through the underbrush. The man's heart raced, and he broke into a sweat as he lay there trying not to breathe or shake. Images of a woman and child flashed through Bone's mind. The man fought the urge to run. Voices came nearer. Twigs snapped.

The air smelled of sweat and liquor. The men were very close. One took a whiz against a nearby tree.

The underbrush rustled. Bone heard the sound of running—and a shot.

She dropped the coin and opened her eyes.

This was her Gift. She couldn't hide from it.

20

HER DADDY WOKE BONE when it was still pitch black out. "Come on downstairs, sleepyhead, I'll make you some breakfast." He tousled her already-wild hair for good measure before he headed to the kitchen.

Bone yawned and rubbed the sleep from her eyes. She inhaled the not-so-far-off scent of fresh brewed coffee, burning toast, and something else she couldn't quite place.

The familiar smell caught in her throat.

He was leaving today.

An icy wave of sadness welled up in Bone, fixing to drown her.

She pushed back the feeling as she fumbled for the clothes Mrs. Price had laid out for her today: her trusty yellow sweater, blue flannel shirt, and corduroy trousers. Her suitcase, packed with her feed sack dresses, overalls, and *National Geographic*s, sat next to the mirror. Bone ignored it for now.

She crept down the back steps to the kitchen in her stocking feet. Daddy stood over the stove, his shirtsleeves rolled up and his pipe firmly clenched between his teeth. The kitchen smelled of burnt toast, cherry tobacco, and scrambled eggs.

Bone tried to stay mad at her father. He was leaving today.

She slid into her chair as he gently slid the pale yellow egg onto her plate. It was the only thing he knew how to make, and he hadn't made them in a very long time. They smelled like butter. Lots of butter.

"I can't remember the last time I made eggs for you." Her father scraped the black off a piece of burnt toast and slathered it with butter.

Bone remembered, but she wasn't mad enough to remind him of *that* evening. She'd never be that mad. It had been the evening her mother died. "You used to make them all the time when Mama was working," Bone said instead.

She took a bite. Her egg melted in her mouth, all hot and buttery. For a moment, things were like they used to be. Bone could imagine it was just her and her daddy, eating eggs, talking about baseball or detective novels. And her mother would be home any minute to join them. Bone stuffed another forkful in her mouth, and the warmth filled up an empty spot in her.

Her father nodded. "I never have figured out how to cook anything else worth a damn." He sat down at the table with his black coffee and toast. No eggs.

"You're not having any?" Bone asked, her mouth full. She'd nearly cleaned her plate and was sopping up the remains with her toast, which he hadn't burnt.

"I've lost my taste for them." Daddy sipped his coffee. His still partly black toast lay untouched. "Who do you think will win the World Series?"

Bone couldn't stay mad at her father.

Especially now. He was leaving, and things could never be like they were. But, for a few minutes, they could pretend.

21

BONE COULD FEEL SOMETHING breaking inside as Daddy climbed into Uncle Henry's black '35 Ford. She bolted after him and banged on the glass.

He was out in a flash, wrapping her in his arms once more. "Honey, I got to go." He pulled away from her gently.

"Daddy, I've got a Gift, like Mama," she blurted out.

Her father let out a sigh. "No, you don't." He bent down to look her in the eye. "Honey, I know what you're doing. You want me to stay, but I can't."

"That's not it." But it was. It was what it all had been about. She'd been clinging to this crazy hope that she could make him stay if she figured out her mother's secrets. Yet Bone couldn't bring herself to ask the sweater, like Uncle Ash said. What if the

Gift did kill her? Bone was more afraid, she realized, of knowing what happened to Mama than maybe losing Daddy. Hope crumbled in her hands like rotten wood.

Her father kissed her on the forehead. "Do not pull this on your Aunt Mattie."

Her aunt and cousin stood up the road, both of them with their arms crossed. Bone felt the water rising around her with nothing left to hold on to.

"She will not think kindly of any talk about the Gifts," he added in a whisper. "I'll call when I get to the induction station," he said in a normal voice. "And send postcards when I can."

And then he was gone.

As the Ford made its way down the road, the taillights disappeared around the bend.

"Laurel Grace Phillips!" Aunt Mattie called.

Bone trudged back up the road to the parsonage, suitcase in hand.

"Well, let's get you settled, young lady," her aunt said, not unkindly. "Ruby, why don't you show your cousin to her new room?"

Bone had been in the parsonage many times over the years, and it hadn't changed much. It was scrupulously clean, with not a feed sack in sight. Everything was store-bought and polished, even the two-way picture of Jesus hanging over the fireplace. If you looked at it from one side, Jesus was riding a donkey, but from the other side he was hanging on a cross. Bone always liked the donkey side better.

Her new room turned out to be Uncle Henry's study.

"Papa didn't put up any fuss when Mama suggested putting you in here," Ruby said stiffly. She ran her fingers through the dust on the bookshelf behind the big wooden desk. "Usually he doesn't let anybody in here."

Most of the room was taken up by the desk and the bookcase filled with Bibles and other religious books. There was an old chair and small closet. A cot was made up under the front window. Bone set her bag down on the cot and perused the stack of magazines by the chair.

"Don't touch Papa's stuff," Ruby said. "You can put your things in the closet. Mama cleared it out for you."

In the tiny closet hung several dresses. They all looked very familiar.

"Mama says you're to wear my old ones." Ruby fixed her hair in the shaving mirror hanging over the closet door. "She bought me all new ones."

"Let's get you unpacked, Laurel," she heard her aunt say from the door.

"I can do that," Bone protested, but Mattie had already swooped in and Ruby was fading away, mumbling something about homework. Miss Johnson had told them not to worry about school today.

Aunt Mattie tsked as she held up the dresses Mrs. Price had made for Bone. "You don't need these anymore. Ruby, bring me that box for the charity clothes drive."

Bone objected again, but her aunt plowed straight ahead. "I told Bay I'd treat you like my own, and I wouldn't let Ruby be seen in those rags." She grabbed the feed sack dresses and about everything else in the suitcase and chucked it in the box Ruby was now holding.

"Not that one." Bone snatched the butter-yellow sweater from the box. "It was Mama's." Bone held it close to her, the lavender and its warmth making her feel less panicky.

Aunt Mattie's eyes narrowed for the briefest of moments. "Yes, I remember that sweater." She turned her attention abruptly to the *National Geographic*s in the bottom of her suitcase. "Laurel, what are you doing with these?"

"Miss Johnson gives them to me."

"Well, I'll have to have a word with Miss Johnson." Mattie leafed through one. She stopped on a picture of a woman in native dress. "These are not suitable reading material for a young lady." As she picked up the last of Bone's belongings and put them in the charity box, something small and hard fell to the floor.

Ruby gasped. It was her arrowhead. Bone had taken it home and stuffed it in her sock drawer, meaning to give it back to Ruby someday. This morning, though, she'd dumped the contents of her drawers into the suitcase without much thought.

"Isn't that yours, Ruby?" Aunt Mattie looked at Bone accusingly. "Didn't you say you'd lost it?"

Ruby had forgotten to tell her mother she'd lost it upside Clay Whitaker's head. Bone smothered a grin.

"Yes, ma'am. I lost it on the playground," Ruby said carefully. "And Bone found it and was bringing it to me."

Actually, Jake had found it.

"Well, pick it up and give it back to Ruby," her aunt said.

The humor of the situation evaporated at the thought of touching the thing again, especially in front of Aunt Mattie.

Ruby made a move to get it, but her mother stopped her. "Laurel needs to learn to pick up things around here. Cleanliness is next to godliness, I always say." She looked at Bone expectantly. Ruby looked petrified. "Well, we don't have all day," Mattie said sharply.

Bone took her mother's yellow sweater in hand and picked up the arrowhead with it. She offered it to Ruby without touching it. Ruby mouthed a thank-you. Aunt Mattie peered at Bone.

"It's sharp." Bone handed it to Ruby. "Didn't want to cut myself," she added—and immediately regretted it. She hadn't meant to remind Ruby of the memory she'd seen, the one of Ruby cutting herself with the arrowhead.

Ruby snatched the rock away from her and threw it into the charity box full of Bone's things from her past life. All Bone had left was her mother's yellow sweater and what she had on. An old flannel shirt, corduroy trousers, and boots.

"Those will do to pull weeds in," her aunt said. "Don't get too comfortable in here," she added. "We've got a lot of chores to do before Henry gets home." She softened a bit. "It'll keep your mind off your daddy."

The first chore was weeding, and Ruby made herself scarce. Aunt Mattie had put in a respectable-looking victory garden in the tiny backyard of the parsonage. She still had a few tomato plants neatly tied to their stakes with strips of flour sacks. The tomatoes looked punier than Mamaw's, or Mrs. Price's for that matter. But the pole beans were growing like gangbusters. Aunt Mattie squatted down to look at them.

Bone's eyes strayed to the back of the garden. There sat what looked like a large white playhouse with a window and lace curtains. The door was padlocked.

"Stay out of my shed," Aunt Mattie said, following Bone's gaze. She thrust a bowl into Bone's hands. "We need a mess of beans for dinner." She stooped to pick a handful and dropped them into her apron.

Bone sank to her knees in the dirt and plucked ripe beans from the vine. The smell of the soil and the lingering scents of the lavender from her sweater made her think of playing in Mamaw's garden with her mother. Bone closed her eyes, and instead of seeing herself, she saw two young girls working and laughing in the garden together. The girls were young Willow and Mattie. When Bone opened her eyes, the older Mattie was staring at her.

"Something wrong with you, child?" Aunt Mattie asked.

"Just thinking about Mama."

Mattie's eyes glistened. "Me, too," she whispered, as she dropped her apronful of pole beans into the bowl.

Bone could see her mama again in her aunt's gray-green eyes. "Why did you and her fall out?" Bone asked.

Mattie stiffened. "I don't know what you're talking about." She brushed the dirt from her hands and stood up. "We need some cucumbers, too," she called over her shoulder as she headed toward the house.

~⁓~

Next, the three of them scrubbed the Alberts' already immaculate house. While Bone did the laundry on the back porch, Aunt Mattie and Ruby fried chicken and mashed potatoes and stringed green beans, all while flipping through movie magazines and talking about such-and-such star's hairdo or figure. The oddest pang of jealousy stabbed at Bone as she watched.

Running wet clothes through the wringer of the washing machine one by one did not take Bone's mind off of much. If anything, it gave her more time to think her thoughts. Where would Daddy be sent? Would it be Africa? Would living with Aunt Mattie be as bad as she thought? Maybe she'd made too much of her in her head. Ruby eyeballed the ingredients as she mixed the dough for bread. She didn't measure a thing, and Aunt Mattie took it all in stride.

The wringer gave out on the washer once, and Aunt Mattie sailed right back to the porch, laid a hand on the offending machinery, tightened a few screws, proclaimed it good to go, and returned to the kitchen in time to flip the chicken.

Uncle Henry took his sweet time getting home, and when he did, it was past supper. Aunt Mattie had held it warming in the oven for him. He had flowers—and smelled of beer. "Now Mattie, I had to buy the man a drink before he left to serve his country."

Bone's father wasn't a big drinker.

Aunt Mattie bit her tongue and put the flowers in the sink. "Supper's ready," she said.

Uncle Henry said grace. At the amen, he hiccuped. Aunt Mattie glowered at him throughout dinner, and Ruby studied her plate as she pushed around her greasy chicken leg.

Aunt Mattie's chicken was not as good as Mrs. Price's, but Ruby's bread was perfect.

"Mattie, Ruby, I've got something to tell you," Uncle Henry broke the uncomfortable silence.

Bone sure didn't like conversations that began this way. Ruby and Mattie looked scared.

He set aside his fork and pulled something out of his jacket pocket. "I got my notice, too." He handed the paper to Aunt Mattie. It looked different than the one Bone's father had gotten. Uncle Henry's was on nice white stationery.

"But Papa, you're a preacher. They can't expect you to fight, can they?"

Bone never thought a minister might get drafted.

"'Army Chaplain Corps,'" Aunt Mattie read from the paper. "'We're pleased to offer you a commission of second lieutenant

172

and request that you report to Chaplain School at Harvard University on September 28, 1942' . . ." In spite of herself, Aunt Mattie seemed impressed.

"But that's so soon," Ruby exclaimed.

Bone counted the days out in her head. Ruby was right, and it seemed awful quick to have to report. Her father had had nearly two weeks' notice.

"Henry, you must have got this last week." Aunt Mattie pointed to the date on the letter.

He nodded. "I didn't want to worry Bayard."

"Bayard? You didn't want to worry Bayard?" Mattie glared at Bone—and then Uncle Henry. "We will talk about this later."

Ruby was wide-eyed.

Bone didn't want to be in his shoes later. She tried to interest herself in her mushy green beans. But Bone stole a look at her uncle. Maybe if Uncle Henry had told her father he'd got called up, too, she'd be sitting at Mamaw's table right now.

Uncle Henry explained he'd be ministering to the wounded most likely over in England. He'd be giving comfort, performing services, and the like.

"What about church here?" Ruby asked, on the verge of tears.

She was trying to find reasons for him to stay, like Bone had done with her father.

"The deacons and elders can do everything I can. Better even. I want to do my part." He pushed a dry piece of chicken under his mashed potatoes.

Aunt Mattie didn't look convinced, and he hadn't heard the last of it. "At least you're going to be an officer. And at Harvard."

Bone felt sorry for Ruby—and Aunt Mattie. But it didn't seem quite fair. Uncle Henry would be in some nice safe hospital in a great big city like London. On the other hand, Daddy would be tromping around in some hot desert in Africa with Nazis shooting at him.

Later that night, Bone lay in the narrow little cot by the window, trying to read one of the detective novels she'd found stuffed under the cot. Bone couldn't help hearing her aunt and uncle's heated whispers.

"What do you mean you signed up?"

"I want to do my part. I want to go where I'm needed."

"What about us? Don't we need you?"

"Amarantha, you've never needed me."

A rap on the door followed, and it opened a crack. "Can I come in?" Ruby asked in a small voice.

Bone was so surprised she forgot to answer. Ruby took this as a yes. Even in the dark of the hallway, Bone could tell she'd been crying. Bone made room for her cousin on the cot.

"Tell me a story." Ruby crawled under the quilt next to Bone.

Bone knew exactly which one to tell her, one she had a newfound appreciation of. "There once was a girl called Ashpet." Bone waited for Ruby to object. She only pulled the quilt more tightly around herself. "She was taken in by a cruel stepmother and two ugly stepsisters who made her do all the chores."

Ruby giggled under the covers. She fell asleep before Bone got to the part about the glass slipper and the king's son.

22

THE MORNING AFTER her father left, Bone pulled her butter-yellow sweater over one of Ruby's old dresses; it had tiny green stripes and a wide white collar. It had been ugly on Ruby, too. Bone was tying her school shoes when Ruby slipped back into the study. She had on a new navy dress that made her look like a sailor. "Ready?" she whispered. "Papa's still asleep, and Mother is getting dressed."

Bone nodded. Ruby wanted to sneak off to school early so she wouldn't have to face her father yet. Bone knew how she felt. She'd been scared and mad at her father, too. Still was.

She and Ruby quietly gathered their books and lunches—and a couple of apples—and tiptoed out the door.

As they ambled up the gravel road, no one else in sight, Ruby finally spoke. "Where do you think they'll send our fathers?"

"Daddy's old unit is in Africa, but he thinks they're moving on to Italy." Bone kicked a rock up the road.

"That doesn't sound as bad as Guadalcanal or the Philippines." Ruby gave the same stone a kick, too. It went skittering off into Mrs. Webb's azaleas.

"Uncle Henry will be fine. He'll be in a hospital or somewhere far away from the fighting." *Unlike Daddy.*

They got to school and sat out on one of the picnic tables. Ruby handed Bone an apple.

She took a deep breath and asked, "Why did you give me that note?"

"What?" Ruby looked puzzled for a second.

Bone stared at her. "How could you forget a note that said *THE GIFT KILLED YOUR MOTHER*?" Bone whispered the last part even though no one else was around.

"Oh, that." Ruby stared at her hands. "I overheard Mother arguing with someone on the phone that morning. I couldn't help but hear it. She was yelling all about how it killed Aunt Willow. And about how it was the devil's work. And she'd take me down to the river and baptize me all over again if she saw the first sign of a Gift in me."

Bone bit into her Red Delicious. Ruby's answer had left so many questions, and Bone wasn't sure where to start.

"But why did you tell me?" Bone finally asked.

Ruby stared at her hands again. "I just wanted to scare you a little," she said in a small voice.

"But why?" Bone stopped chewing.

"I could see you had a Gift that day we found the arrowhead." Ruby pulled it out of her pocket.

"How did you know?" Bone bit into her apple again. Why did Ruby rescue that stupid arrowhead from the charity box?

"Mamaw tested me on my birthday. Don't tell Mother! Uncle Junior told her we were going to Radford to get some ice cream. We did that after we saw Mamaw."

Mamaw had asked her some questions and then had Ruby touch some plants, an object, one of the cats, and Mamaw to see if she felt anything. "Mamaw said those were the most common Gifts in the Reed family, but sometimes the Gifts skip people. Like Mother. Maybe me."

"You're lucky." Bone rubbed her arm. She'd give almost anything to not have this Gift. Almost. She could still see Tiny Sherman's shattered arm, but she could also still feel Papaw's joy in running out on the field and smell the lavender that trailed after Mama's love. She didn't know what to feel about it all.

"I don't know about that," Ruby muttered. She tossed her apple core out past the johnny house.

"But how can one of those Gifts kill a person?" Bone whispered. She could see Miss Johnson and Miss Austin walking up the road toward the schoolhouse.

"I don't know, Bone," Ruby said, exasperated. "I've got other things on my mind." She gathered up her books and went inside.

Bone bit into the last of her apple.

"Glad to see you two are finally getting along," Miss Johnson told Bone.

Bone hoped that was true. But she couldn't help wondering if it suited Ruby to be friends now that her father was leaving, too. She tossed her apple core in the trash and followed the teachers into school.

❦

After school, Bone didn't wait for Ruby. She ran up to the store where she found the faded yellow pickup truck waiting for her. Even though Daddy was gone, she still wanted to know—no, she needed to know—what had happened to Mama. Bone wanted to visit Queenie, but Uncle Ash said he didn't care to—and that was that. So they collected several stories from an older lady who lived along the river road. She'd been one of her mother's patients but didn't have anything new to add to what Bone already knew. Maybe Uncle Ash was right. Maybe this wasn't the best way. Maybe she should use her Gift on the sweater. Bone shook herself. No, she couldn't, not yet. What if the story was as awful as Tiny Sherman's arm? Or the deer? Bone did not want to feel Mama die.

Uncle Ash and Miss Spencer let her off outside the parsonage gate.

It was 5:30 p.m. The lace moved in the front window.

"Where have you been, young lady?" Aunt Mattie greeted her with the question—and a wooden spoon—as soon as Bone opened the front door.

Uncle Henry peeked over the top of his paper and then snapped it back into place. The sound of chopping echoed in the kitchen.

Her aunt waved the spoon in Bone's face.

"Story collecting with Miss Spencer," Bone said. "We do it every afternoon."

"Who gave you permission to do that? I certainly did not." Aunt Mattie's hands were on her hips now.

"Daddy did." Bone felt the smack of the wooden spoon on her backside.

"Don't answer back, young lady."

"Mattie!" Uncle Henry folded his paper. "Bay did say she could go with Miss Spencer."

Aunt Mattie shot him a look that shut him right up. Then she turned that look on Bone. She wished she had a newspaper to hide behind, too.

"You are to come straight home after school."

Bone didn't say anything. She figured she could take a paddling if it meant going out with Uncle Ash and Miss Spencer.

Aunt Mattie's eyes narrowed. "And to make sure you do, I'll keep this ugly thing." She pointed to Bone's butter-yellow sweater. "Take it off."

"It was Mama's." Bone wrapped her arms around herself.

"You can earn it back."

Bone wasn't going to budge.

Aunt Mattie pulled an envelope out of her apron pocket. "From your father."

Bone reached for it, but Mattie held it above her head. "The sweater."

Bone reluctantly peeled it off and handed it to Mattie.

"Now go help Ruby with dinner."

Bone ripped open the envelope. Inside was a scrap of paper wrapped around a fifty-cent piece. *For a better movie* was all Daddy wrote. It was hardly a fair trade.

Bone didn't see where Aunt Mattie stashed the sweater.

She had a feeling she'd never earn it back.

23

BONE WASN'T SURE he'd come, not to Mattie's house, but Will was a creature of habit. The knock on the back door came right as she was putting away the last dish.

Bone scrambled to open the door before Aunt Mattie heard.

"I am so glad to see you, Will Kincaid," Bone whispered—and shooed him back out onto the little half-covered porch. The Alberts' house didn't have a proper porch you could comfortably sit on, either in the front or the back. This one was made more for work than leisure. The wringer washing machine and a laundry tub took up most of one side of the porch. A bare bulb hung over a stool on the other side. Bone turned over the tub for him, and she took the stool. Will kept standing. Bone didn't blame him.

"How's the mine without Daddy?" Bone tried to sit ladylike on the stool in Ruby's castoff dress but failed utterly. Will tried hard not to smile.

Busy, Will scribbled out on his pad. *Not enough men. How's it here?*

"Busy." Bone nodded toward the washing machine. "I think I've wrung every piece of clothing in the house through that thing since I got here. At least I got to go to school today."

Heard about the preacher.

"Yeah, Uncle Henry leaves in a few days. Aunt Mattie ain't too—"

The kitchen door flew open. "What in the Sam Hill is going on out here?" Aunt Mattie demanded.

"Will just stopped by to talk. He always came by the boardinghouse—"

Mattie cut her off. "You're not at the *boardinghouse* anymore." She said it like Mrs. Price's place wasn't respectable. "You are not to entertain boys out here in the dark. What will the neighbors think?"

"We can sit in the kitchen."

"No, you cannot," Aunt Mattie said shrilly. "You are too young to entertain boys period."

"It's only Will." Bone was baffled. She figured Aunt Mattie would be stricter than Daddy, but this was Will. She always talked to Will after supper.

"Will is a young man. He works for a living, and you ought to act like a young lady," Aunt Mattie explained. She made it sound so reasonable. Just like Daddy.

Will nodded. He started to write it out for Bone. She didn't want to see it.

"But Will is my friend, my best friend," she pleaded.

"You can see him in church," Aunt Mattie said. "Now go do your homework and get ready for bed."

Will motioned for her to go on and turned to go himself.

"Yes, ma'am." Bone stalked back into the house.

But she didn't go to her room. She hovered by the back door, listening.

"You wait just a minute, Will Kincaid," she heard Aunt Mattie say. "You stay away from Laurel. I don't want to even see you passing your little notes to her in church. She's under my roof now. My rules. I don't want her associating with the likes of you or your raggedy miner friends."

The porch was so silent Bone could hear the 8:15 chugging along the tracks down by the river. Then Will's boots stepped off into the grass and trudged away.

Bone planted her feet, ready to take on her aunt.

"Go to your room, young lady," Aunt Mattie said without even opening the door. Her footsteps disappeared into the yard, too.

Bone waited a moment and then cracked open the back door. The yard was dark—except for the light on in the shed.

24

BONE CAME STRAIGHT HOME after school the next day. A half hour later, Uncle Ash honked out front. She peered through the lace curtains. He and Miss Spencer and Corolla sat outside the parsonage's white picket fence in the faded yellow Chevy. Bone grabbed her coat and headed toward the door.

"Where do you think you're going, young lady?" Aunt Mattie asked not at all like a question.

"Uncle Ash and Miss Spencer are outside." She'd done what her aunt had asked. She had to let her go now.

"I heard him honk like white trash," Aunt Mattie said evenly. "I don't want you running around with them anymore. You've got chores and homework."

"But Daddy said—" Bone was cut short by a knock on the door. She went to open it, but Aunt Mattie stared her down.

"Amarantha?" Uncle Ash asked from the other side.

Aunt Mattie finally opened the door and faced her brother. "Laurel will not be accompanying you and your lady friend on your little jaunts around the county. And I'd appreciate if you didn't honk outside my house and park that dilapidated jalopy where everyone can see."

"Mattie." Bone could hear the exasperation in Uncle Ash's voice. "You know Bone has been helping Miss Spencer with her government work. You also know that Bayard approved of that."

Ruby appeared in the kitchen door and waved a little wave to Uncle Ash.

"Bayard left her with me. I promised him I'd take care of Laurel like she was my own. And I certainly wouldn't let Ruby run around with you." Aunt Mattie spat the words at her brother.

Uncle Ash looked downright hurt.

"And you promised Bayard you wouldn't interfere once he left." Aunt Mattie drove her advantage home. "So I'd advise you to steer clear of *my* girls for the duration." She slammed the door in Uncle Ash's face.

Bone and Ruby stood absolutely still. After a few moments, Bone heard Uncle Ash's boots leave the porch, and the engine of the old yellow truck faded slowly down the road.

"How could you do that to Uncle Ash?" Bone finally asked.

"Do not sass me, young lady," Aunt Mattie said in a low voice.

Ruby grabbed Bone and hustled her to her room before Aunt Mattie turned her fury on either of them.

As they sat on her cot not saying a word, Bone felt cut off from everyone. Daddy. Will. Ash. The river was rising all around her, and Aunt Mattie was slashing any rope thrown to her.

Bone was overcome with the desire to bury her face in the comfort of her mother's butter-yellow sweater.

When Aunt Mattie went off to visit parishioners, Ruby helped Bone look for the sweater inside the house. Bone had to admit it was nice to have Ruby on her side for once. She wouldn't go in Aunt Mattie's room, though. Bone secretly vowed to search it at her first opportunity. They didn't find anything Bone hadn't already seen except an old hatbox stuffed at the bottom of the hall closet. They took the hatbox into Bone's room. Inside, there were old photographs wrapped in tissue. The yellowing paper tugged at Bone to unwrap it. As she did, the warmth came off one picture in particular. It was an old-timey photograph, and the two children in it were posed in their Sunday best. The older girl, who was probably about Bone and Ruby's age, held a toddler in her arms. On the back, written in Mamaw's familiar scrawl, were the date 1906 and the names Amarantha and Willow Reed. Bone could feel the pure love coming off the photograph. There was a later photo of the two sisters. This one was dated 1929. Her daddy had a copy, too. Willow Reed sat there in her nursing student uniform, trying to be all serious, but the mischief shone through her eyes. Bone could feel a mixture of emotions off this one. Pride for one. Disappointment for another. And anger. She caught a flash of Aunt Mattie getting this picture out every once in a while and thinking about how things might have been.

"Can you read those photographs?" Ruby asked. "What do you see?" Ruby leaned in.

"It's complicated," Bone answered. "But your mother loved mine."

"I know that, silly," Ruby said. "I mean, what do you *see* when you touch the photos or an object?"

"With some things, it's like watching a movie. With others, it's like being thrown into the movie all of a sudden." Bone gingerly wrapped the pictures in the tissue and put the hatbox back in the hall closet.

"But what's it *feel* like to have a Gift?" Ruby persisted.

Bone shrugged. She didn't know how to put that in words. And she hated when people insisted on knowing how she felt.

"Does it make you feel, I don't know, special?" Ruby wouldn't let it go.

"It scares me," Bone finally said. "And yeah, maybe I do feel a little bit special," Bone admitted. "But I'd rather be good at math or baseball or something useful."

"No, you wouldn't," Ruby said. She got up from the cot and smoothed out her dress in the mirror.

"Anyway, I still can't figure out how the Gift would kill anyone, though." Bone changed the subject. "Tired maybe." Bone stretched out on her cot. This whole thing was making her feel weary.

"Maybe *my* mother was wrong." Ruby turned to Bone. "Maybe she was jealous of your mother."

Bone sat up. *Ruby envied her.* Bone would have never believed it in a million years. But she knew why now. "Mamaw told you that you don't have a Gift, right?"

Ruby nodded.

"Maybe Mamaw is wrong." Bone had a hunch both Ruby and her mother had Gifts that they were not aware of. "Maybe you haven't been in the right situation yet," Bone added, reminded of her grandmother's words. *Junior didn't think he had one at all until he went down in the mines.*

Ruby tiptoed to the door to listen for her mother. "Neither of them likes to admit it when they're wrong." Ruby laughed a rueful little laugh. "The last time Mamaw was here they had a big old fight. Mother told Mamaw never to darken her door-step again."

"When was that?" Bone couldn't remember Mamaw ever visiting the parsonage.

Ruby thought for a long second. "It was right after Mother was sick with the flu—and Aunt Willow was here taking care of her," Ruby said slowly, as if the memories were trickling into her head from long ago. "Daddy had sent me to stay with Mamaw. We came back when . . . your mother died . . ." Ruby trailed off.

"Mama died here?" Bone croaked.

"I thought you knew," Ruby whispered. "I think that's the last time Uncle Ash was here, too."

"What else do you remember?" Bone eyed her cousin narrowly.

Ruby racked her brain for a moment, and then shook her head. "Mama was screaming something at Uncle Ash. Daddy took me over to the church. But I could hear her clear over there. Mama was out of her head with grief or fever or both."

"What was she screaming?" Bone whispered.

"'Fix her,'" Ruby said quietly. "What does it mean?"

Bone shook her head, but she was beginning to put it together. If only she had her yellow sweater to nudge her along.

25

UNCLE HENRY LEFT Thursday morning. It was only a two-
day trip to Boston, but the northbound Greyhound only left
on certain days. Aunt Mattie drove him to the bus station while
Ruby and Bone walked to school. Ruby sniffled all the way there,
while the other Jewels moped behind. Pearl's father had gotten
his notice, too. School was quiet. Almost every man (or boy) of
fighting age from Big Vein was either already off to war or on his
way there. Bone couldn't help feeling like it was only right that
everyone's father should be off fighting like hers. But she kept
that thought to herself.

That evening, Uncle Junior came to dinner, and he brought
his old battered guitar.

Bone set the table while Ruby tested her corn bread with a toothpick.

"Please, Junior, not tonight." Aunt Mattie set the green beans and fried chicken on the table.

"What? You don't want me to sing for my supper?" Junior cleared his throat and threatened to strum the strings.

Aunt Mattie relieved him of the guitar, placing it in Uncle Henry's chair in the sitting room. "I will pay you *not* to sing." Aunt Mattie stuck a piece of the corn bread Ruby had sliced into Uncle Junior's mouth.

"You got a deal, Sis," Junior said through a mouthful of corn bread.

Aunt Mattie laughed.

Mattie and Junior got on like a brother and sister should. Of course, it was hard not to like Uncle Junior. But Aunt Mattie was always so mean to Uncle Ash—and everyone else. It hadn't occurred to Bone that her aunt liked anyone, not even Uncle Henry. Now Uncle Junior was making her laugh. Ruby cracked a smile, too.

During dinner Uncle Junior talked about the goings-on at the mine. They were combining first and second shifts because there weren't enough men. That meant, though, they might have to work longer hours to meet the quota.

"You're still going to be in charge, aren't you?" Mattie asked. "You deserved to be supervisor long ago."

Uncle Junior shifted a little uneasily, glancing at Bone. "Bayard is a heck of a lot better at this leadership stuff than I am. He can have this job soon as he gets back."

Aunt Mattie harrumphed into her glass of sweet tea but didn't say anything more on the subject.

"Will's doing real well, Bone." Uncle Junior helped himself to another drumstick. "He's a natural-born coal miner. I think he actually likes it."

"He does." Bone stuck a forkful of mashed potato in her mouth.

"Do not speak with your mouth full," Aunt Mattie told her. "And remove your elbows from my table."

Her aunt's good humor vanished. Ruby intently picked at her burnt chicken thigh.

Uncle Junior made a big show of taking his elbows off the table. Aunt Mattie wasn't amused.

"Mattie, do you and the girls want to go to the ball game Sunday? It's the last one of the season. Great Valley versus Merrimac."

Bone and Ruby exchanged hopeful glances.

"I've got a vestry meeting after church," Mattie replied, her lips tightly drawn into a smile that wasn't one. "Henry left a lot of things undone." She moved the green beans around her plate with a fork, separating the little onions into one pile and the beans into another.

"I could take the girls," Uncle Junior offered.

Aunt Mattie cut him a look. "They've got Bible study." She stabbed a bean with her fork.

Bone's hopes for a brief escape were dashed.

Uncle Junior pushed away his plate and put his elbows back on the table. "Girls, can I talk to my sister for a moment?"

Bone sprang to her feet, but Ruby hesitated.

Aunt Mattie nodded. "You all get started on the dishes."

Bone and Ruby quickly gathered up the dinner plates and hustled into the kitchen. Ruby turned on the tap, but they both listened at the door.

"Amarantha, it's okay to let them out of your sight and have a little fun," Uncle Junior said gently.

"What they do is my business, Hawthorne." Her voice was still flinty sharp.

Ruby smiled, and Bone almost joined her. It was hard to think of Uncle Junior by his given name.

"Well, you had no business speaking to Ash that way, Mattie." Uncle Junior was sounding more like the older brother now. "Bayard wanted Bone to help that Miss Spencer, and I'm sure he wants her to see her family—all of it."

"So, is that what this whole visit is about? Laurel and Ash? You are always taking up for that mess of a brother. And here I thought you'd come to cheer me up on account of my husband going off to war."

"I am here for you, Mattie, if you'll let me." Uncle Junior was back to trying to soothe his sister's temper. "I want us all to get along like a family should. And Bone and Ruby and you need all the family you can get. Mama would be over here in a shot if you—"

"I . . . we can do without all you heathens' help," Aunt Mattie sputtered. "You know, it wouldn't hurt you none to come to church more often. And just because your girls have grown up and moved away from you doesn't mean you can come interfering with mine."

Uncle Junior was silent, but Bone could hear a chair pushing away from the table. "Well, I guess I'd better go," Uncle Junior said.

"Girls, come say goodbye to your uncle."

Ruby dashed to the sink to turn off the water.

Bone and Ruby tiptoed into the dining room. Aunt Mattie grabbed the rest of the plates and walked straight as a rod into the kitchen. At that moment, Bone could see a bit of Mamaw in her aunt.

Uncle Junior hugged Ruby and Bone. And then he was out the front door, taking Bone's hopes for a smooth evening with him. His guitar was still on the chair in the sitting room. Bone grabbed it, and at once was flooded with love. Junior was serenading Aunt Vivian while they were courting. He could not sing a lick. Bone barely remembered her, but Junior's giddiness made Bone grin. She pushed the vision aside and ran after Uncle Junior. He was standing by the front gate, trying to light a cigarette in the moonlight. He'd quit smoking years ago. But a fresh pack of Chesterfields was poking out of his shirt pocket.

"Thanks, Bone." He coughed as he took the guitar from her.

"Why does she hate Uncle Ash so much?" Bone suspected it had to do with what Ruby had remembered, but neither of them could quite make any sense out of it.

"Honestly, I got no idea. They were never that close, but after Willow died, Mattie took it out on everyone, especially Ash." Uncle Junior shrugged. "Maybe Ash reminds her of Willow too much. I expect you do, too."

"Is it because of the Gifts?" Bone asked.

"That's why she tolerates me." Uncle Junior grinned a bit. "She thinks I'm thoroughly ungifted in so many ways. But I think it's mostly to do with Willow's death."

"What really happened?"

"Neither Mattie nor Ash will say boo about it," Uncle Junior said quietly.

Ashes grew at the end of her uncle's forgotten cigarette.

"Most folks say it was the war that changed Ash. It did but it wasn't the only thing. Losing Willow hit him just as hard." Uncle Junior tried another puff on the cigarette—and coughed again. "How does he smoke these things?" Junior shook his head. "The two things Ash don't like to talk about are the war and Willow. Both are still fresh wounds to him. I got to get him drunk to even say two words about either." Uncle Junior stopped and looked at Bone. "But you, Bone, might get him to open up about both. Someday."

Uncle Junior tossed his barely smoked cigarette on the ground and crushed it to bits with the toe of his boot. He pecked her on the cheek, slung the guitar over his shoulder, and strode off to his shack up the hill. The full moon hung over the side of the mountain, lighting his way.

Bone sighed. It might be easier to get the moon to open up and spill its secrets than it would Uncle Ash.

26

BONE ELBOWED RUBY as they walked home together after school, trailed by the Little Jewels, Opal and Pearl. None of them were in a hurry. The weather was still warm, the leaves were turning dark reds and oranges, and the goldenrod was in full bloom along the gravel road. And they all had chores to do, Bone and Ruby especially. Aunt Mattie had them cleaning house, collecting scrap metal, working in her victory garden, and even sweeping out the church when they got done with homework. With all that, Bone still hadn't found her sweater, but there were two places it could be. However, Aunt Mattie was always at home, rarely leaving the house these days without taking Bone and Ruby with her.

"Isn't that Mamaw?" Bone asked.

Across from Flat Woods, a silver-haired figure in a black jacket and dungarees was stooped over by a tall patch of goldenrods. When she straightened up, Mamaw tied a string around an armful of the tall yellow flowers and stuffed them in the basket hanging from the crook of her left arm. Bone ran down the road to meet her grandmother. Ruby didn't follow. She stood up the road, with Opal and Pearl looking on.

"Y'all come on," Bone called.

Ruby glanced back toward the parsonage before saying goodbye to the other girls. She walked slowly at first, but then broke into a run. Mamaw scooped her up like she had Bone.

Bone spied a yellow truck outside the boardinghouse.

"He's visiting with Miss Spencer." Mamaw strode toward the parsonage. "I was coming to see you all—and Mattie."

Ruby stopped in her tracks. "I don't think that's a good idea, Mamaw." She peered at her house.

The lace in the front window moved.

"I come to make peace," Mamaw said. "I even brought a little offering." The basket on her arm held zucchini, yellow squash, and sweet potatoes from her garden. And something wrapped in checkered cloth smelled like bread. She tucked the long-stemmed goldenrods under her arm. "These are for my patients."

"What do the goldenrods do, Mamaw?" Bone asked.

The three of them stopped outside the parsonage's white picket fence. Mamaw handed Ruby the basket and took out the flowers. She held them in her hand like she'd held the burdock root that day in her cabin. She closed her eyes for a moment.

"It reduces swelling. It's good for gout and arthritis." Mamaw opened her eyes. "And I recently saw how it could help with kidney stones."

Bone was thirsty for more. She wanted to know more about the Gifts, and she wanted to talk over the clues she'd gathered and the visions she'd seen with Mamaw. All of it was roiling around in her head like a whirlpool.

"Mamaw," Ruby whispered urgently. She flicked her eyes toward the front porch.

Aunt Mattie was standing there, arms crossed, glaring at them. "What do you think you're doing, Mother?"

"I come to visit my daughter and granddaughters." Mamaw opened the front gate. She waved Bone and Ruby through with the goldenrod still in her hand. "Brought you some of that squash you like so much."

"We have a garden," Aunt Mattie answered stiffly. She eyed the plump-bottomed, bright yellow squash in the basket Ruby was holding. The squash growing in the parsonage Victory Garden out back was puny and pale in comparison.

"Amarantha, we need to bury the hatchet, you and I." Mamaw paused on the bottom step, looking up at her daughter. When she didn't budge, Mamaw asked, "Can I at least come in for a cup of coffee?"

Aunt Mattie glanced up and down the row of houses before stepping aside.

Mamaw settled herself down at the kitchen table, laying the flowers to one side. "Put those vegetables in the sink, Ruby," she said. "And wash them good."

Bone tiptoed over to the sink to help Ruby. Together they began to rinse the squash and zucchini, moving slowly and quietly so as not to disturb the potential powder keg behind them. Bone lifted a sweet potato; it still smelled of the earth up on Reed Mountain. It filled Bone with longing to be there. Or anywhere but here.

"Have you heard from Henry yet?" Mamaw asked.

Aunt Mattie poured her mother a cup of coffee from the pot on the stove. She didn't pour herself one. She leaned against the kitchen counter with her arms crossed. Bone couldn't see her aunt's face, but she could feel the icy glare directed at Mamaw. Finally Aunt Mattie said, "He wrote when he got there. He said they were shipping out to England in the next day or so. Apparently, chaplains don't need much training. Just pop them in a uniform and put them on a boat . . ." Aunt Mattie's words caught in her throat.

Ruby's head snapped up, and she looked at Bone. She shook her head slightly. Evidently Aunt Mattie hadn't told her. Bone heard a chair move and peeked behind her. Aunt Mattie sat down across from Mamaw.

"Oh, Mattie. I'm sorry, hon." Mamaw reached for Aunt Mattie's hand, but she drew it away.

Bone turned back to scrubbing the sweet potatoes. Ruby sniffed back a tear, and Bone leaned into her so their shoulders touched. Ruby leaned back.

"I'm here to help you and the girls anyway I can," Mamaw said softly.

"Where have you been the last six years?" The chair scraped across the floor, and Aunt Mattie sprang to her feet.

Bone and Ruby stood stock-still, the water running over their hands. Trapped. It was going to be like dinner with Uncle Junior, only Mamaw was probably a fair match for Aunt Mattie.

"Girls, go do your homework," Mamaw said.

Bone didn't need to be told twice. Neither did Ruby. They escaped to Bone's room, leaving the door open so they could listen.

"Amarantha, you're the one who kicked me out. But that don't matter. I shouldn't have stayed away. I wanted to respect your wishes."

"Everything is still always my fault, isn't it, Mother? Is it my fault I wasn't blessed like you and Willow and Ash?" Aunt Mattie said the word *blessed* like it was anything but that. "Was it my fault I got the influenza? Was it my fault that Willow—" Aunt Mattie broke off.

"I never said any of it was your fault, Amarantha, especially about Willow."

"You never want to blame what's really at fault. You never blame the—" Aunt Mattie said the last word so quietly that Bone could only guess what it was. *Gifts.*

"Honey, the girls know about the Gifts."

Bone and Ruby exchanged a wide-eyed look.

"What?" Aunt Mattie roared.

"And they need to know how to handle them . . . if they're so gifted."

"What did you tell them?"

"You can't protect them from what's inside of them, Amarantha."

"Me and the Lord certainly intend to do just that." Bone heard feet stomping across the kitchen and the front door opening. "And you know Bayard agreed with me. That's why he gave me Laurel. I want you out of my house."

It was quiet for a long moment, and Bone wondered if Mamaw had left. What did Aunt Mattie mean about it not being her fault? A chair pushed back from the kitchen table, and Mamaw's boots moved slowly across the floorboards. "Amarantha, I know you feel like I never take your side. But I meant what I said about burying the hatchet. If you and the girls need anything, I'll be here in a heartbeat."

The front door slammed shut.

Bone dashed out of the study and ran after her grandmother.

"Bone, don't!" Ruby called quietly after her, but she didn't follow.

Luckily, Aunt Mattie's bedroom door closed with another bang. Bone eased open the front door and caught up with Mamaw at the front gate.

"What did Aunt Mattie mean?" Bone asked, clinging to the gate. "Was it her fault?" She whispered the last part.

Mamaw shook her head. She looked weary, like she'd gone five rounds with a heavyweight champion and thrown in the towel. "No, Bone. She thinks I blame her because she lived and your mama didn't."

Bone relaxed her grip on the pickets and opened the gate.

The horn of the old yellow truck honked as Uncle Ash drew up beside them, just him and Corolla in the cab. "Hey, how's my Forever Girl?"

Mamaw dropped the goldenrods she was still holding and leaned a hand against the truck to steady herself. Bone scooped up the flowers.

"You okay, Mama?" Uncle Ash bolted out of the truck, but Mamaw waved him off.

"I'm tired. You know how talking to your sister can be."

Uncle Ash gave Bone a look, and she helped her grandmother into the truck.

"Yes, indeed, I do." He slid into the driver's seat. "It's like beating a rug with a broom—only you're the rug." He winked at Bone. "Does Mattie still make her calls on parishioners on Wednesdays?" he asked out of the blue.

Bone nodded. Her aunt always checked on the parishioners that didn't live right in Big Vein at the same time every week.

"Hang in there, Forever Girl." Uncle Ash threw the old truck in gear. It protested, but Ash whipped it around and headed back toward Dry Branch.

The little yellow truck disappeared up the road in a cloud of whirling dust. Bone felt like she was clinging to a tree to keep herself afloat in the raging water, watching a ship speed away from her.

27

AFTER SCHOOL WEDNESDAY, Aunt Mattie took Ruby to do their calling on parishioners. They'd call on as many as the gas rationing would allow. They'd left Bone with the cleaning and laundry. She scrubbed the floors and dusted and swept as fast as she could, hoping to at least be able to go outside. The house was beginning to close in on her, and Bone felt every inch like Ashpet.

But the empty house and the chores gave her a chance to think—and find her sweater. Bone pushed open the door to her aunt's room. The curtains were closed tight, and the room was a dark cavern. When Bone flipped the light switch on, the view didn't improve much. The room was sparse with only a four-poster bed, a chest of drawers, and a tiny closet. Bone carefully looked through the closet. Mattie had a handful of nice dresses. Uncle Henry didn't even leave a suit. It was like he'd never lived here. And there was no yellow sweater.

Bone crossed the creaking hardwood floors, pausing in the empty spot next to the bed. It would've been perfect for a big chair. Bone felt dizzy and sad standing there for even a second. She hurried away from it.

On the dresser, the picture of a grim-faced Mattie and Henry in their plain wedding clothes stared at Bone. Next to Mattie stood Bone's mother, holding the wedding bouquet and beaming. There was no yellow sweater in the picture—or in the drawers. But there was a key, and the only place Bone hadn't searched was Aunt Mattie's padlocked shed.

Bone grabbed the key and made a beeline for the shed. She tried to peek through the windows as she fumbled with the lock, but the lace curtains didn't reveal anything. Bone figured it would be full of gardening tools, potting soil, and perhaps a push mower. When she opened the door and pulled the string on the bare light bulb, Bone's jaw hit the ground. Inside, the shed was roomy and bright—and decorated. The walls were painted a pale yellow with white trim. A large, comfy chair occupied one end, and neatly arranged and labeled shelves took up the other end. But in the middle was a long table, a workbench really, with old radios and clocks and other gadgets in various states of repair spread across its surface. A rack of hand tools—screwdrivers, wrenches, and the like—hung on the wall. Their outlines had been precisely painted around them in blue to show exactly where each one went.

Aunt Mattie had a workshop.

Bone ran her fingers over a radio and then a pair of pliers. She felt a tingle of happiness. Her aunt contentedly tinkered with a clock, the radio softly playing Glenn Miller in the background. And she was talking to someone—or something—off to the right. Bone glanced over and saw it. Her butter-yellow sweater was hanging neatly on a hanger to the side of the workbench.

She pulled her sweater down and inhaled its scent. It still smelled of lavender.

She saw Mattie and Willow as young girls playing in the creek down below the Reed tree house. Mama couldn't have been much older than Bone. Mattie fell and cut her palm wide open on a rock. The wound gushed, and Mattie cried out. Her little sister took the bloody hand in hers. "See what I can do." Willow held Mattie's hand for a moment and then washed it off in the water. There wasn't a mark to be seen.

Her face white as a ghost, Mattie stared first at her hand and then at her sister.

Mattie's eyes widened, and her mouth opened in surprise. "Oh, Willow, I thought you could just *see* what ails people." She wrinkled her nose, her upper lip raised in disgust. Mattie leapt up, backing away from her sister. "Never, ever tell anyone you can do *this*." She held out her pristine palm. "Not even Mother.

Or Ash." Her eyes narrowed. "It's the devil's work," she hissed before stalking off.

Mama could heal.

Mama felt small and hurt, and it wasn't something she could heal herself.

But she still loved her sister.

Bone liked her aunt not one little bit.

She pulled on her sweater. She felt bathed in happiness to have it back. And yet she was boiling inside. How could her aunt have taken this away from her? How could she have turned her back on her own sister?

A knock on the shed door made Bone jump. It was Will. Freshly scrubbed from the change house. He must have known Aunt Mattie wasn't home.

He peered into the shed with an amused look on his face. "It's Aunt Mattie's."

Will motioned up the road toward the store.

"Let me get my coat." Bone didn't need any more convincing than that. "And put this back." She held up the key. She'd put it back—but not the sweater. It was hers.

꜆꜒꜈

On the way up the road, Bone was still thinking about everything she'd seen. Will nudged her, and she shrugged. Then she asked him how the mine was going with Daddy gone. Will shrugged back.

He was leading them up to the store. Mr. Scott was sitting on the front porch, smoking and talking to Uncle Junior and Uncle Ash. This is why Ash asked about Wednesdays. Bone felt like crying she was so happy to see all of them. She might make it through the week if she met Will and her uncles every Wednesday.

"There's my Forever Girl," Ash drawled. Corolla bounded down to greet her. The other dogs were curled up at Ash's feet. "Got you a Nehi." He indicated the empty rocking chair between him and Junior.

"Will, that radio you ordered for your mama come in yesterday," Mr. Scott said, pushing himself to his feet.

Bone sank gratefully into the empty chair between her uncles and took a long satisfying drink of her grape soda. "Which of ya'll planned this jailbreak?" She looked at Uncle Junior.

Uncle Junior laughed and pointed at Ash.

"Now how would we know that Amarantha was calling on folks down toward Parrott?" Uncle Ash asked a little too innocently.

"Well, we can't have Mattie keeping you under a washtub, Ashpet," Uncle Junior said. Ashpet's stepmother hid her under a washtub every time company came to call.

"Uncle Junior!" Bone didn't want this particular nickname to stick—even if it did fit.

Will wrote out quickly, *The house is awful clean.*

"It was clean to begin with." Bone sighed and took another drink of her Nehi. Ash offered her a peppermint stick. It was just what she needed.

The sun warmed Bone's face as she sat with Ash and Junior and Will in the crisp fresh air. She unbuttoned her coat. Her uncles talked easily about the mines, with Will contributing his thoughts here and there on his scraps of paper. They asked her about school and Ruby. Uncle Ash said he'd come over to see to a lame horse and deliver some packages for Mamaw.

"Uh-oh," Uncle Junior interrupted. A black Ford was stirring up the dust on its way toward them. "She can't be done with her calls yet."

"Gas rationing." Uncle Ash groaned. "Without Henry here, I bet she don't get as many points."

"I'm done with my chores. Almost," Bone added the latter quietly. She didn't budge from her chair. She was still mad about the sweater—which she was wearing. Bone buttoned her jacket to the top.

The Ford pulled up next to the yellow Chevy pickup in front of the store. Aunt Mattie got out of her car, straightened herself like she was heading into battle, and steamed up the steps.

Ruby, trailing behind, waved to Ash and Junior behind her mother's back.

"I'm going to see if that fabric I ordered came in," Mattie told her daughter. She didn't acknowledge Will or her brothers, but she froze when she saw Bone sitting between them. "Laurel Grace Phillips. What are you doing here? Are you finished—"

"Now, Amarantha," Ash began.

"Now nothing, you. I told you to stay clear." She shook a finger at her younger brother. "I am talking to Laurel. She had chores to do."

"Mattie, it's our doing," Junior interrupted her, but she did not want to be interrupted.

"I trusted you and left you on your own, young lady, to take care of your responsibilities. And this is how you repay me?" Aunt Mattie's voice crackled. "I am terribly disappointed in you, Laurel. I took you in—"

Bone was simmering inside. Ruby wouldn't look at her.

"Mattie, that is enough," Uncle Junior's voice rang out. He rose up out of that chair like a great tree and glared down at his sister.

Usually Uncle Junior reminded Bone of that thick braided wire that pulled the ferry across the river or the mantrip up from the mine. The towline didn't look like much from afar, but it was tough and near unbreakable and much more complicated up close. Today he seemed like one of the giant oaks that held up the Reed house.

Uncle Ash pulled himself out of his chair and stood shoulder to shoulder with his older brother. Both of them crossed their arms and waited for their sister to say another word.

Mattie spun on her heel and stormed back to her car. It wouldn't start. But before the men could move a reluctant muscle to help, she whipped out of the driver's seat, threw open the hood, jiggled a wire, and then fired up the engine. "Get in the car, Ruby," she growled, and then they were off down the road again.

The brothers exchanged a glance.

"Henry did not show her that."

"No, he did not," Ash replied.

Junior looked thoughtful.

"Come to supper?" Ash asked him.

"No, I think I'll stick around." His eyes trailed up the road.

"Suit yourself." Ash nudged the dogs awake with his foot and pointed them toward the truck. "You better get home, Forever Girl. We'll arrange another jailbreak soon." Ash kissed her on the forehead before he lit himself a cigarette and shook Will's hand goodbye.

"Uncle Ash? Why does Aunt Mattie hate this sweater?" Bone unbuttoned her coat so that the yellow peeked out. It was easier to ask than some of the other questions she had.

"Aw, Forever Girl. I think that sweater has seen too much." He kissed her again and hurried down the stairs to his truck.

Bone buttoned her coat back up.

⁓

Will seemed to have his mind elsewhere as they walked slowly back to the parsonage. And Aunt Mattie certainly didn't invite him in. She barely even acknowledged Bone. Ruby was out of sight. Mattie was intently chopping up vegetables for dinner. Quiet fury radiated off her, and Bone made herself scarce, too.

⁓

Bone hung up her coat in the tiny closet in the study then rushed to finish making up the beds. Everything was swirling around in her head as her hands went through the motions of her chores. Had Mattie and Willow parted ways over healing that cut? Did Mama never tell anyone else about her true Gift, that she could heal? Had she healed Tiny? And how did her Gift kill her? What had the sweater seen? That's twice Uncle Ash had said something about it.

Bone was putting clean towels in the hall closet when she heard Aunt Mattie yell at her, "What the hell do you have on?"

Bone had been so wrapped up in her thoughts about the sweater that she'd forgotten to take it off. Still. She turned on her aunt. "*My* mother's sweater," Bone said, emphasizing the "my." Bone's anger boiled over. "That you stole and hid in your shed."

Ruby emerged from her room and stared at her mother.

"Give it here," Mattie said.

"No, it's mine. It's all I have of Mama."

"I do not want to see that sweater again." Mattie measured out every word.

"She'll take it off, Mother," Ruby said carefully, like she was calming a stray dog. She turned to Bone, with pleading in her eyes, but Bone was tired of appeasing Mattie.

"If you don't want to see this sweater, then you better not look in my direction," Bone blurted out. "'Cause I'll be wearing it."

Aunt Mattie moved faster than Bone thought possible. The woman grabbed a great handful of fabric at the nape of Bone's neck and yanked on it with all her might. The cardigan ripped down the back, about taking her shoulders off in the process. Bone was left with just the sleeves, which fell to the floor as Bone stood there in shock. Mattie threw her handful of butter yellow at Bone's feet.

Bone sank to her knees and scooped up the fabric, trying to will it back together. Without thinking, she closed her eyes and held the soft wool to her cheek. The images hit her like a cold splash of water, waking her up from a long sleep. She saw a new memory; this time Mattie was there. Bone's mother was laying the sweater across her sister as she slept. No, she was sick, really sick.

"Mama put this across when you were—" Bone wanted to say *dying*, but then she opened her eyes and looked into her aunt's face.

Aunt Mattie's eyes were the size of saucers, and she was incredibly still. Then in a flash, she grabbed Bone's hair and dragged her down the hall. Bone fought the rising panic as Aunt Mattie push-pulled her toward the bathroom like a rip current toward a rock.

"Mama, what are you doing?" Ruby cried out.

"Run the cold water," Mattie commanded Ruby. "You've got the devil in you," her aunt told Bone.

Bone struggled, but her aunt had an iron grip on Bone's hair and neck. Ruby didn't move, so Mattie dragged Bone to the tub and turned the water on herself.

"Mama, don't," Ruby begged over the sound of running water. "You don't know what you're saying."

"She's got the Gift just like her mother." Mattie ranted about the Reed Gift and quoted some Bible verse about casting out demons.

Bone's fear rose with the water level.

"Don't," Ruby sobbed. Aunt Mattie was unreachable now.

She yanked Bone over the edge of the tub and pushed her head toward the water.

In the distance, Bone heard Ruby running toward the door. "I'll get help, Bone."

"I baptize thee . . ."

Bone's face hit the ice-cold water. The shock of it took her breath away. It was like that buck drowning in the icy currents of the New River.

Mattie held her there for what seemed like an eternity. Bone scrabbled at the sides of the tub. She tried to push herself up, but her aunt was too strong. Panic filled her—and then Mattie pulled her head up. Bone gasped for air, groped for something solid to grab onto.

"In the name of the Son . . ."

Mattie shoved Bone's head back down into the icy water.

Bone tasted the iron bathwater sliding down her throat. Aunt Mattie was going to baptize the life out of her if she didn't do something fast. She tried to push herself up again, but the tub was too slippery. Bone's arms flailed in the water. She grabbed for the stopper, but her aunt pulled her head up before Bone could get her fingers around the plug. Instead, Bone elbowed her aunt hard, and Mattie's grip loosened enough for Bone to squirm free. She scrambled toward the door of the bathroom over the wet tiles. Mattie lunged for Bone's foot, but she slipped and sat down on the floor hard.

Bone locked eyes with her aunt, and, in that instant, Mattie blinked.

"Oh lord, Bone, I'm sorry." Her eyes looked like Mama's again.

Bone didn't trust it. She took off running through the front door and stumbled out onto the gravel road, heading toward the river. Mattie called after her, and Bone ran even faster. Then she heard Uncle Junior's voice, "Amarantha, what the hell have you done?"

Bone kept going. It was dark and beginning to rain. Her hair and shirt were soaked through, but she wasn't feeling the cold yet. She wasn't feeling anything—other than the desire to be as far away as she could from Big Vein. Maybe the ferryman was still there. It would be a long walk to Mamaw's but she'd done it before. Or maybe she'd walk clear to Radford or Roanoke or hop a freight train to somewhere else.

She was shivering by the time she reached the river. There was no ferry. No boats. No nothing but more icy water. She stood on the dock and waited.

Soon, though, she heard footsteps running toward her on the gravel road.

"Bone," Ruby cried out. She wrapped Bone in her coat and gently dried her hair with a towel. When she was done, she stood shoulder to shoulder with Bone. "We'll go to Mamaw's together."

Bone was as numb as if she'd fallen in the New River in January. The two cousins waited side by side for the ferry that had already stopped running for the evening.

28

WILL AND THE BOYS found Bone and Ruby huddled together on the dock in the gently falling rain. Everybody had heard the commotion and gone out to search for them.

Uncle Junior kept an eye on his sister until one of the church ladies could come watch her.

The cousins spent the night curled up in Bone's old bed at the boardinghouse. Bone felt like the weight of the mountain had lifted off of her as she heard Uncle Junior and Mrs. Price and Miss Johnson murmuring together into the wee hours. Ruby shivered and tossed in her sleep. The weight was still on her.

Bone awoke to the smell of eggs and biscuits and mint tea and the sound of gentle laughter and country music coming from downstairs. Bone found Mamaw and Uncle Ash in the boardinghouse kitchen when she crept down the stairs to avoid waking Ruby. Mrs. Price was peeling some potatoes that the Reeds had probably brought from their garden stores. Uncle Ash was leaning his chair back, smoking and telling Miss Spencer one of his devil dog stories. Both had a plate of eggs in front of them.

Bone was at home for the first time in what felt like forever.

"Hey there, Forever Girl." Ash jumped to his feet and closed the distance between them. Mamaw wasn't far behind.

"Is Ruby still sleeping?" Mamaw asked.

Bone nodded. Her cousin had been having nightmares all night.

"Hungry?" Mrs. Price asked.

"Ravenous," Bone croaked out as she sat down to a heaping plate of scrambled eggs, fried potatoes, and jelly biscuits. Mrs. Price always felt the generous application of food could put right most problems. Mamaw set a steaming cup of minty tea in front of her. Mamaw felt the same about teas and tinctures. "This will make you feel better." She kissed the top of Bone's head.

For once, Bone didn't feel like talking. She shoved forkful after forkful into her mouth, warming herself on the food and the company. She was hungry for both. She hadn't had anything to eat since that Nehi and peppermint stick Uncle Ash had given her at the store—before Aunt Mattie laid into her.

Mattie. Bone could still taste that cold bathwater.

All of a sudden she couldn't eat another bite. Memories of the cold water and not being able to breathe washed over her.

"Do I have to go back?" she asked, fighting the shivers.

"No!" every single person in the kitchen told Bone at once.

"You can stay with us," Mamaw said.

"I'll drive you to school every morning," Uncle Ash added.

"Or you can stay here in your old room," Mrs. Price said. "Junior said he's going to move in until Bay gets back. And we'll all look after you."

"You don't have to decide now, honey," Mamaw said. "But I want you to know you always have a place to go."

"But what about Daddy? He wanted me there . . ."

"I'll write him. He never would have wanted you there if he thought Amarantha would . . ." Mamaw trailed off.

Bone took a sip of her tea, and it warmed her back up.

"What about me?" Ruby asked from the doorway.

Mamaw swooped in and hugged her. "You've always got a place to go as well," she told Ruby as she held her granddaughter's face in her hands.

"Is Mama okay?" Ruby asked quietly.

"Mrs. Linkous is with her now. I'm going to make them a plate and take it over," Mamaw said. "Do you want to go with me?"

Ruby nodded. Mamaw made her sit down and eat first.

Bone certainly did not plan on seeing her aunt anytime soon. And no one even asked her if she wanted to go, which suited her fine.

"So what's on your agenda, Forever Girl?" Uncle Ash asked. He was going to drive Mamaw and Ruby over to the parsonage and then make some of his own calls. Animals that he needed to see.

"Not a thing." Bone smothered a cough. She was content to stay right here. She'd been plucked out of the raging river on the point of drowning—literally—and now she was high and dry on shore, sunning herself on a log.

"I could use some help, Bone," Miss Spencer offered.

They spent the rest of the morning sorting stories and indexing them according to subject and area and teller. Miss Spencer even gave her a lesson in shorthand. And they made lunch for themselves out of biscuits and mint tea. They talked about college, ancient Rome, and movies. Bone felt safe and free and full of possibilities—and possibly a little sick. But she didn't let on.

In the afternoon, Ruby came back with Bone's suitcase in hand.

"You're staying with her, aren't you?" Bone asked, a sinking feeling in her gut.

"Mama needs me. She says she's awful sorry." Ruby pulled a flat package from her coat. "You should have this."

Bone unwrapped the brown butcher paper. Inside was her sweater, dry and clean and in one piece. Neat seams joined the pieces together invisibly.

"Mamaw helped me fix it while Mother slept."

Bone hugged the sweater to her chest, breathing in the lavender. She could hear her mother softly singing.

"What are you going to do?" Ruby asked.

Bone shrugged. It didn't matter as long as she wasn't *there*.

"Are you going to be okay?" Bone wrapped the sweater back up in the paper.

It was Ruby's turn to shrug. "Walk me to school tomorrow?"

Bone nodded. She followed her cousin out onto the porch. It felt like solid ground underneath her feet as she watched Ruby slowly make her way up the river of gravel to the parsonage. Bone wished she had a lifeline to throw.

⁓

That evening there was a familiar rap on the back door. Bone had set out a piece of pie and a glass of milk for him. She read the new *National Geographic* Miss Johnson brought home for her while Will ate at the kitchen table. This issue was all about North Africa, where her father was soon to be.

"I'm fine," she said. "Mostly," she added in answer to his very loud thoughts. She wasn't quite ready to talk about it, even with Will.

After Will drained the last drop of milk, he ushered Bone out onto the back porch. As she was about to sit on the steps, Will dropped to one knee and handed her a slip of paper.

Marry me, it said.

Touching the paper, she could see his vision of them growing old together in a tiny cabin by the river.

"I'm only twelve, you fool," Bone said as kindly as possible. "And you're only fourteen." She tried not to laugh. She loved

Will, but she wasn't sure it was in *that* way. She wasn't even sure what *that* way was.

I know, he scribbled out. *In a few years. Just want to protect you.*

"Thank you, Will Kincaid." Bone kissed him on the forehead and then pulled him to his feet. "But I think I might want to go to high school, and maybe even college, first."

I'll be here.

I know, she scribbled back.

"You didn't really think I was going to say yes, did you?"

He shook his head. Bone knew he'd been serious in his own way, but he seemed content. He was always content. And she felt better for the asking, but she didn't need a prince to save her.

Tell me a story?

She told him the tale of Jack and the Doctor's Daughter until she could talk no more.

29

BONE WOKE UP ALONE in her room at the boardinghouse, fully intending to go to school. She dressed in the only clothes she had left that Aunt Mattie hadn't foisted upon her even though the corduroy pants and flannel shirt needed a wash. The yellow sweater hung over the door, but Bone was reluctant to put it back on just yet.

Mrs. Price was cooking oatmeal in the kitchen, and Uncle Ash and Miss Spencer were talking over the paper.

"You feel up to going to school this morning?" Mrs. Price asked.

"I'll run you up there," Ash volunteered. "It's raining cats and dogs. The road's beginning to wash out."

School was never canceled in Big Vein on account of weather. You either got there or you didn't.

Bone opened her mouth to answer but nothing came out. Not even a hoarse whisper. She kept trying to say something. Anything.

Uncle Ash nearly laughed. Miss Spencer elbowed him before he could. Not that Bone could blame him. Bone Phillips, teller of stories, could tell no stories this morning.

Mrs. Price laid the back of her hand against Bone's forehead. "She does feel warm. I better send for Dr. Henderson."

Dr. Henderson, the closest doctor around, lived in Radford.

"I'll get Mama." Ash pulled himself up and threw on his coat. "She's staying at Mattie's until things calm down."

What Uncle Ash meant was until they were sure Aunt Mattie wouldn't crack again and maybe go after Ruby this time. Bone wasn't sure Mattie hadn't gone after Ruby before, even though Ruby had denied it when Mamaw asked her.

Bone sighed and dug into her oatmeal. She didn't feel too sick, but she was sure glad to stay home for a while.

"I'll make you some of Mother Reed's tea," Miss Spencer said. "It's probably good for laryngitis."

Bone wished she had a pad and pen, but she didn't even think she could spell that word.

"Laryngitis means you lost your voice. It happens when you talk too much or you get sick. The vocal cords get inflamed," Miss Spencer explained.

"It's no wonder. You were soaking wet and chilled to the bone when the boys found you," Mrs. Price said when she returned from calling the doctor. "He'll be over this afternoon, if he can. In the meanwhile, it's hot liquids and bed rest for you, young lady."

Mamaw agreed with the doctor's prescription when she came over a little while later. She spent the morning plying Bone with herbal teas with honey, both of which Ash fetched from their home up the mountain, despite the river rising.

~ ⁊ ᵕ

Dr. Henderson arrived after lunch and pronounced that she did indeed have laryngitis. He sniffed at Mamaw's teas and said they couldn't hurt and to call him if she wasn't better in a few days.

Bone nodded off reading her *National Geographic* over the murmurs of Mrs. Price's favorite soap opera, *Against the Storm*, playing downstairs.

The yellow sweater still hung over the door.

Bone dreamt of drowning in a sea of yellow yarn, with only Mattie's face peering down at her from above.

30

BONE AWOKE TO THE BANGING of the screen door, boots clomping, and male voices laughing in the kitchen. She crept down the stairs in her pajamas to see what the commotion was all about.

Will was holding open the back door for Uncle Ash and Uncle Junior. Both of them had their arms loaded up with grocery boxes full of clothes, books, and pictures. And Will had Junior's beat-up old guitar in his hands.

"How's my Forever Girl?" Uncle Ash asked as he plunked a box down on the kitchen table.

Better, Bone mouthed. She wasn't sure she was.

Corolla scrambled across the linoleum floor toward Bone.

"I told you boys to be quiet, or else you'd wake her up," Mamaw scolded. She was pouring hot water into yet another pot of herbal tea. She motioned to Bone to sit at the table. "Let me get you something to eat, child. You slept through supper."

"Let's take these boxes to your room, Junior." Ash scooped up the box he'd set down. Junior grabbed the guitar from Will, and the brothers headed upstairs.

Bone slipped into her old seat at the kitchen table. Mamaw poured a cup of peanut soup for Bone and set a glass of milk and a piece of spoon bread in front of her. The smells flooded her memory. She could see her mother serving this exact meal whenever she was sick.

"Eat," Mamaw told her with a remembering smile. "You need something on your stomach."

Got a present for you, Will scrawled out on a scrap of paper. He dug in his pocket for a pad of paper with a little pencil tied onto it. It was like the ones she'd given him.

Very funny, she scribbled back.

Her uncles' boots clamored down the stairs, and the screen door slammed as they headed out for more boxes.

"They're like a herd of elephants." Mamaw shook her head. "As you probably figured out, Junior is moving into your daddy's room until he gets back."

Bone sipped the nutty, buttery soup, and it warmed her down to her toes. Having Uncle Junior around would almost be like having Daddy back, almost like having things the way they were. Almost.

I want to stay here, if you don't mind, Bone wrote out and handed it to Mamaw.

She nodded. "I'll be here every day to check on you."

Uncle Ash burst into the kitchen. "Mama, there's an army man knocking on Amarantha's door."

"Oh lord." Mamaw sprang to her feet.

"Junior run up there to see." Ash held the door open for his mother.

As she moved past, Mamaw laid a hand on Bone's shoulder. "You two stay here."

What does it mean, Bone was busy writing out.

"It's your Uncle Henry," Uncle Ash answered.

The door banged shut, leaving Will and Bone in their silence.

⁓

Bone was thankful Will didn't leave. He turned on the radio in the boardinghouse parlor. She heated up the dregs of the coffee for him and cut him a slice of apple pie. The newsman broke into *Fibber McGee and Molly* to announce that an American troop transport ship had been sunk in the North Atlantic by the Germans. Roughly two hundred soldiers and sailors lost their lives.

Maybe the preacher survived, Will wrote.

Bone pulled out Daddy's map and studied the North Atlantic. It was vast and deep.

An hour or so later, Ash and Junior returned. Bone looked from one uncle to the other. Uncle Junior sank into the leather chair by the fireplace. Uncle Ash shook his head wearily before collapsing on the sofa in the parlor.

Uncle Henry had not survived.

Bone's heart quietly broke for Ruby—and perhaps even a little for Aunt Mattie.

31

THAT EVENING, Bone lay in bed unable to sleep. So many things kept rolling around in her mind. She couldn't quite put them all together. The sweater still hung on the closet door, waiting for Bone. Her mother had been nursing Aunt Mattie—and covered her up with that sweater when her sister was dying. But she didn't—and Willow did. Bone could understand Aunt Mattie a little better now. Mattie loved her sister, but she knew she could heal. She hated it. And she feared it, too. Had Mama tried to heal Mattie? Is that what killed her? What happened in those few hours?

Only the ordinary butter-yellow sweater knew.

Bone groaned. There was nothing for it. She had to see what it was, but she was still afraid. What if those moments were even more awful than the dinner bucket or the arrowhead or Tiny's ball cap? These ordinary objects bore witness to the lives unfolding and dissolving in front of them, and if the moment was charged enough, the object took it all in like a silver plate in a photograph. But she was the only one who could see it.

How had she not seen this awful thing before? Then Bone remembered what her Mamaw had said about her Gift. The plants would show her something new when she studied on them. Their secrets were always revealing themselves, if only she asked them to.

Her own Gift was more complicated. Plants didn't have as many secrets as ordinary objects. They were more like people. Some wore their sadness and pain right on the surface, their jagged edges sharp to the touch. Others clothed themselves in love and happiness. Yet, the ghosts of sadness and pain might hide deep within them. The deeper ghosts revealed themselves if Bone asked, if Bone was ready.

Bone had to ask. Bone had to know. Bone was ready. And it was for her to find out, she decided. This was her Gift. What had Uncle Ash said earlier? *You ask that sweater of yours. It saw everything.*

Bone slipped out of bed and stood before the closet door. She laid her trembling fingers on the sweater once more and dove into the river of images.

The happy, familiar times hit her first. Her mother tending her arm when Bone fell out of the tree. Her mother singing "You Are My Sunshine," rocking baby Bone to sleep.

Then she saw her father proposing to her mother in his army uniform. He wasn't much older than Will, and her mother couldn't have been that much older either. Bone had forgotten how lovely she was. Tall and lithe and freckled. This soft object had witnessed nearly all the important moments of her mother's life.

Bone wanted to linger there in this little eddy of happiness. She could feel the cool currents of sadness underneath, but the happy was stronger in this place.

Bone pushed out into the current.

She saw her mother sitting on the bank of the creek, watching her sister run away from her. Willow Reed picked up a rock and sliced her own hand open. She held her hand over the cut and closed her eyes. The wound didn't heal.

Bone dove deeper.

She saw her mother in Aunt Queenie's house. A young Tiny Sherman moaned on the kitchen table. Uncle Ash and another man held him down. Mama yanked his arm straight, and Tiny screamed. She splinted up the arm and gave him a tincture for the pain. The men carried Tiny into the bedroom. Bone's mother sat by his bed. When no one was looking, she held her hands over the worst of the breaks. The bones knitted together. Tiny stirred, and Mama went home with her brother—and slept for a day and a half.

Bone swam farther.

Mama was sitting by someone in the bed. It was her sister Mattie, feverish and still. Mama coughed as she laid her hand on her sister's forehead and closed her eyes. Bone could feel her mother's Gift. She was searching for the disease in her sister's body, and she saw it burning up Mattie's veins. But there was more. Bone could feel Willow willing the sickness to go away.

It did. But only from Aunt Mattie. Her mother had already caught the influenza—and couldn't heal herself.

Mattie's eyes flickered open and she spoke. Mama took off her sweater, beads of sweat forming on her flushed face. *"You'll be fine now, Mattie,"* Willow said. *"Sleep."* She laid the butter-yellow sweater over her sister like a blanket and tucked her in.

Bone felt the tug of the story; it wasn't over, though she didn't want to know the rest.

Mama slumped in the chair beside her sister.

Mattie awoke later to find herself covered by the sweater—and her sister dead in the chair, in that empty spot in her room, where Willow Reed Phillips had closed her eyes for the last time. Uncle Ash was sitting on the floor beside her, weeping. Aunt Mattie screamed at him for being useless. For not being able to heal like Willow. For not being able to fix their sister.

No wonder Mattie hated the sweater. Bone could almost forgive her aunt. Almost.

Her heart broke into tiny pieces for Uncle Ash.

Bone wiped her eyes on the sweater. Aunt Mattie had been right. Not about the devil. About her mother's Gift killing her. Mama could heal. She healed Mattie. But the healing had made her weak, too weak to fight off the influenza. She couldn't heal herself, and Uncle Ash couldn't heal her either. It wasn't his Gift. Aunt Mattie still blamed him, though. Blamed him, Willow, and all the Gifts for what happened. Daddy and Mamaw were right, too. Willow simply caught the influenza from someone she'd nursed. It took her real quick. Many people, including Mattie and Mr. Childress's wife and Opal's little sister, came down with it. Mama had tended them all, but she'd only healed one of them.

Her sister.

And Aunt Mattie hated everybody and everything for it.

Bone felt drained herself, but she wasn't ready to sleep. Not yet. She scrambled to find some paper and a pencil in her room. When she did, she stared at the whiteness and didn't know where to begin. So she wrote down everything.

Someone else needed to hear the story.

32

"I FIGURED IT OUT," Bone croaked as she handed the paper to Uncle Ash.

He and Corolla had brought her a tray of fried bologna sandwiches—with mustard just like she liked them—and a Nehi. "You missed breakfast."

The little dog hopped up on the bed and eyed the plate expectantly. Bone grabbed the grape soda, gratefully letting the cold drink slosh down her still-scratchy throat. She didn't think she could stomach another mint tea.

"You got your voice back, Forever Girl!" Uncle Ash shooed the dog off the bed and sat down in her place.

Bone smiled. "Barely," she whispered and pointed to the

papers. She couldn't say all that out loud, even if she had her full voice. "I asked the sweater."

The color drained right out of Uncle Ash's face. "You did?" His voice was creaky now.

Bone nodded.

He swallowed hard as he read, and his hand began to shake a bit. Bone couldn't watch. She tried a bite of her bologna, but she wasn't hungry. She threw it to Corolla instead. The little dog gobbled it down. Uncle Ash didn't even look up.

Bone could see the story play out on his face. His eyes widened at the part about her mother healing her sister when they were young. "She never told me," he whispered, hurt clear in his voice.

His eyes closed when he got to the end. Finally, he spoke, "That was the day I saw the black dog outside Mattie's. I went running in. Both of them looked asleep. I checked Mattie to make sure she was still breathing. Willow was curled up in the big old chair Mattie keeps by the bed. She had an angelic smile on her face, like she was dreaming of better days." Uncle Ash's voice caught. "Well, I guess she was." A single tear rolled down his cheek. "I put my hand on her shoulder to wake her up. I was going to take her home, but she was ice to the touch. I lost it then and there. I don't remember much after that. Next thing I know Junior is driving me and my truck up the mountain so we can tell Mother." He took a deep breath and let it out slowly. He fumbled with the pack of Luckies but didn't take one out.

Tears were welling up in Bone, for Uncle Ash and Aunt Mattie mostly. Mama had saved her sister, yet it had wrecked her and her brother both. But that wasn't Mama's fault.

Bone inhaled the lingering lavender of her mama's butter-yellow sweater. She'd found her mother deep in that pile of yarn—and deep inside herself, a river flowing through her like a gift.

"Aw, Forever Girl, yours ain't an easy Gift." Uncle Ash cleared the way between them. He folded Bone in his arms, the sweater crushed against her. "Thank you," he whispered.

Bone cried a river. So did Uncle Ash.

Corolla ate the fried bologna sandwiches, crusts and all.

33

A BANG CAME FROM THE KITCHEN. Bone found Mrs. Price putting a pound of flour and a pound of salt into a box.

"Pounding for the Alberts," Mrs. Price said, dry-eyed.

According to the army man, Uncle Henry's transport ship had been on its way to Greenland, a staging area for troops going to England. When the U-boat struck, Henry and three of the other chaplains gave up their life jackets so that others might be saved. The memorial service would be tomorrow at the church. Henry Albert was receiving a Silver Star posthumously. He had done his part.

Bone's father called from Fort Benning that morning. He couldn't come home because they were fixing to ship out in a few days, but she was sure glad to hear his voice. Mamaw had written him about what happened. Bone wished Mamaw hadn't. Daddy had enough to worry about, with the Nazis and all. "I'm awful sorry, Bone, I never thought . . ." His voice broke. "Of course, you can stay at the boardinghouse with Junior."

Bone hadn't talked to Aunt Mattie since that night.

Mrs. Price put a pound of navy beans into the box.

"I'll take it over," Bone said, her voice back to normal.

Mrs. Price hesitated. "You don't have to, you know."

"I know." Bone still wasn't quite ready to forgive her aunt, but she was family. And there was Ruby. She'd just lost her daddy. "Let me get one thing." Bone ran up the back stairs.

On her dresser lay the butter-yellow sweater, the power of its story still radiating off it. Her mother had given it to her sister out of love in her dying moments. There was more love in the object than death, more happy than sad.

Her mother was in there, and she still had the power to heal.

Bone stuffed her mother's sweater into the pounding box and walked through the drying mud and leaves to tell her aunt a story.

Author's Note:
Story Sources

I based Bone's world on that of my grandparents during World War II. I never knew my grandfather, Richard Scott. He died a month or so before I was born. He and his brothers worked in the coal mines and minded their father's company store in McCoy, Virginia, a tiny village by the New River. One of the mines in McCoy was called Big Vein and the other Great Valley. For the sake of this story, I simplified the geography a bit and perhaps took a few artistic liberties here and there. Some of my historical sources for the period include *McCoy, Virginia Remembered*, a privately published scrapbook put together by one of the local churches, and *Appalachian Coal Mining Memories*, a compilation of oral histories of miners collected by Radford University. (The latter includes two interviews with my grandfather's youngest brother, Leo "Scotty" Scott, who was also a semipro baseball player.) Bone's world existed until the 1950s when the mines petered out and closed.

Bone's world was also squarely in the Southern Appalachians (pronounced with a short *a*, as in "latch"). This area has a rich tradition of storytelling. The stories in this book—including several Jack tales, "Ashpet," Ash's devil dogs, and "Forever Boy"—are adapted from authentic Appalachian and Cherokee folktales. My sources include the Virginia Writers' Project, the work of folklorist Richard Chase, a collection of Cherokee tales by Barbara Duncan, and Ferrum College's AppLit site.

From 1937 to 1942, the Virginia Writers' Project collected stories and interviewed people throughout the state, including Southwestern Virginia. Part of President Franklin Roosevelt's Works Progress Administration, the VWP put writers and teachers to work preserving history and traditions of both black and white Virginians. In 1943, VWP records were sent to the University of Virginia library, where they sat until the 1970s. Eventually, the stories were published in *Virginia Folk Legends* in the early 1990s.

In the 1930s, Richard Chase collected Jack tales and other Appalachian folklore—including "Ashpet"—from residents in western North Carolina. Most American and English readers are probably familiar with "Jack and the Beanstalk." In Appalachia, Jack had many, many other adventures. Chase published these stories in several volumes, including *The Jack Tales* and *Grandfather Tales: American-English Folk Tales*.

Long before Bone's (and my) ancestors settled in the Appalachians, they were the home of the Cherokee as well as many other Native American tribes. The Eastern band of the Cherokee remained in (or in some cases returned to) western North

Carolina after the Trail of Tears. "Forever Boy" and other stories of the Little People were collected in Barbara Duncan's *The Origin of the Milky Way.*

One of my first sources for both Appalachian and Cherokee tales was Ferrum College's AppLit (Applit.org) site. It's a great resource for readers and teachers of Appalachian literature for children and young adults. Dr. Tina Hanlon has compiled a wonderful list of literature, bibliographies, folktales, songs, poems, lesson plans, and so forth of the region. She also pointed me toward other sources, such as the Duncan book. Many thanks, Tina!

And a special thanks to my local critique group, my agent, Susan Hawk, and my editor, Rebecca Davis, for believing in Bone.

In *Lingering Echoes*, the second book in the Ghosts of Ordinary Objects series, Bone struggles with the aftermath of her near-drowning at Aunt Mattie's hands and seeks to learn more about her Gift. Then Will brings her a mysterious object to read . . .

THE FAMILIAR RAP on the back door came as Bone opened the icebox.

She slipped on her sweater and joined Will on the back porch, two cool chocolate oatmeal cookies in her hand. The crisp air outside was like the tart taste of green apples. Airish, folks would call it.

Hester Prynne, Miss Johnson's tabby cat, wound her way through Will's legs as he sat on the step. Animals loved silent Will Kincaid. If Uncle Ash were still here, his dogs would be lying at Will's feet, too. Bone pressed a cookie into his hand and plopped down beside him.

She bit into hers. It wasn't as sweet as usual. More oatmeal than cocoa, but still good. She asked him how work was. He knew what she meant. He always did.

He scribbled out something on his little notebook. *Beat. Five cars today. Army upped the quota.*

"I bet Junior is already snoring away in Daddy's chair," Bone said. Uncle Junior was now Will's boss, the day shift supervisor, since Daddy was off to war. Just for the duration, Junior always added. He'd moved into the boardinghouse just for the duration, too. Bone had a feeling the duration might be longer than she'd thought.

Will wrote something else. *Don't mind. More money.*

Bone nodded. The men got paid per carload. And war needed coal. Loads and loads of coal. For the duration.

He handed her another cocoa-smudged page. *Something odd happened today.*

"Nobody got hurt, did they?" She licked the cocoa off her fingers.

Will shook his head as he wrote. *No, it were during lunch.*

Bone took the slip and watched him as he wrote out a bunch more in his pocket-sized notebook.

I sat down in the cut like usual. Pulled out my pie and biscuits— and this.

He reached into his coat pocket and revealed an empty jelly jar. He set it between them.

She could imagine him sitting on the dirt floor of the mine, his mining light on, spreading out his dinner on a kerchief. Pecan pie. Ham biscuits. Slaw. His mother was a good cook.

You'll never guess what was in it.

"Apple butter." Fall was when everyone churned and canned dark, delicious apple butter. Bone could almost taste it slathered onto a hot biscuit.

Will shook his head.

Edgar Bergen & Charlie McCarthy

Bone stared at the words. They made no sense at all. "What

in the Sam Hill are you talking about?" she asked finally. How could a radio show be in a jelly jar?

Will carefully opened the jar just a smidge and held it between them. Sure enough, Bone heard a funny voice say something and then an audience laughed before Will screwed the lid on tight.

"Wait! Was that the dummy?" Bone felt herself going wide-eyed. Charlie McCarthy was Edgar Bergen's ventriloquist dummy. "Do you mean the jar . . ."

Will nodded.

He set the jar back down between them—and inched it toward her.

Bone knew what he wanted. She held her hand over the jar. She could feel warmth radiating off it, like there was an ember or even a coal fire banked down deep inside it. And it was pulling at her. She had a strange feeling, too, one she couldn't put a finger on. This was like nothing she'd ever felt, Gift or not. She snatched her hand away. "I am not touching that thing."

Will put his hand over the jar, protectively. Bone wasn't sure if he was protecting her or it.

"Was that in your daddy's dinner bucket?" She'd gone with Will to get his mining gear at the store. She'd seen darkness and black earth and timbers falling on Will's father—before Will snatched the tin bucket out of her hands. That's what his daddy's gear had witnessed in the moments before his death. But this jar was different. It wasn't just a witness. It was something more. And it scared her.

Will was writing something out—on several slips of paper.

"I need to get you a bigger pad," Bone joked uneasily.

He ignored her, handing her the first slip.

Yes, the jar was in Daddy's bucket.

He handed her another slip.

The first time I opened it, I swear I heard his voice.

Bone looked up at Will. He nodded.

"Why didn't you say something then? That was nearly two months ago." Bone was peeved that he'd kept this to himself.

Will shrugged and handed her several slips.

Thought I was hearing things. And the jar hasn't made a peep since then. It's always had something in it. Jam. Pudding. Apple butter. Today, the jar was empty.

Bone allowed how he might think he'd imagined a voice. "Why Bergen and McCarthy?"

He handed her the next slip.

Mama listens to it when she makes my lunch on Sunday.

He let that sink in.

"So you're saying this jelly jar catches sounds?" This was wilder than any story she could think up.

Like lightning bugs in a mason jar.

Will had caught her one of the last lightning bugs of the season. Summer in a jar, she'd thought. She'd put it by her bed, but its light was gone by morning.

"You know that's as crazy as I don't know what."

About as crazy as you reading stories in objects. Will grinned. He'd known exactly what she'd say.

"You want me to read this thing, don't you?"

Will shrugged, but his face said yes. His eyes longed to know.

Bone inched her hand toward the jar again. She could feel its pull. It had a power, a Gift maybe, all its own. Without even touching it, Bone could see little flickers of images. Will Sr. and a very young Will were fishing. The jar was between them, filled with worms. Young Will turned to his daddy and said, "*Knock, knock!*"

Bone snatched her hand away again—and tucked it under her leg.

Will could speak!

She peered at him in the darkness. Bone couldn't recall him ever talking. Some folks said he spoke before his daddy died. Bone was barely walking back then. "Do you remember when you stopped talking?" she asked.

Will stared back at her, his eyes searching her face for a clue. Finally, he shook his head.

"I'm not touching that thing. Not yet anyways."

Will looked away. Bone felt lower than dirt.

"But I got an idea."

His eyes snapped back to her.

"Write down all the things you miss hearing down in the mines. Sunday after church, we'll hunt us up some sounds to put in that jar."

Coming March 2020